DOWN AMONG THE
DEAD MEN

Stephen glanced over the side, down into the stack where the grid was fixed, almost afraid of what might be lying there.

And then he saw it.

A dark shape crumpled beneath him, its limbs thrown out at unnatural angles in ungainly, sickening fashion. There was neither sound nor movement . . .

Books you will enjoy
from Keyhole Crime:

DOWN AMONG THE DEAD MEN

Evelyn Harris

KEYHOLE CRIME
London · Sydney

First published in Great Britain 1979 by
Robert Hale Limited

Copyright © Evelyn Harris 1979

Australian copyright 1981

This edition published 1981 by
Keyhole Crime, 15-16 Brook's Mews,
London W1A 1DR

ISBN 0 263 73657 1

Made and printed in Great Britain by
Cox & Wyman Ltd., Reading

One

Someone was standing at his elbow. If he had not heard the whisper of feet upon the gravel, the sudden shadow which blotted out the sun across his closed lids would have been warning enough. Stephen kept his eyes firmly shut.

"Mr Brand ... Mr Brand ..."

He ignored the call, and a gentle patting began on his arm; a regular drumming like summer rain, light, but growing progressively more insistent.

The voice spoke again, a childish treble that kept time with the relentless tapping hand.

"Mr Brand! Mr Brand!"

"Go away," muttered Stephen drowsily.

The hand paused for a moment in mid-pat before continuing its drum beat, and evidently the figure beside him moved a fraction because the sun once more fell across his face, hot and flame-red against his shuttered lids.

"Please, Mr Brand, wake up ..." The voice was beseeching, and reinforced again by the tapping hand. Stephen, recognizing both, wrinkled his nose.

"Rosalind Taggard ... Go away!" From the East to Western Ind ... and upwind, too, he thought idly. Why, in heaven's name, couldn't the Taggards have a good wash occasionally? This one smelled of smoke and grease and onions, and something more subtle but less easily identified. "I'm asleep, Rosie. It's Sunday afternoon, a time of rest – for those who should be so lucky! – and nothing and nobody is going to prise me from this chair." He opened a lazy eye. "Or don't you care that I've been giving my all for weeks?" The fact that he was the newest member of Mr Chapworth's junior staff, and the rector's future son-in-law, to boot, had ensured that not only had he been actively involved in all the preparations for the pageant of the day before, but also that he had spent the whole of the following morning clearing up the resultant debris.

The child beside him shuffled her feet.

"It's Dix, Mr Brand."

"Yes. It would be. It usually is." Stephen allowed his eyelid to droop again. Dix. Dixon Taggard, aged six, whom yesterday he could have throttled with his own tie. Probably would, one day –

"So – what has Dixon done now?" he queried sleepily.

"He's missing, Mr Brand."

"Then no doubt the village is counting its blessings."

"Mr Brand –" The voice shrilled directly into his ear, and warm breath fanned his cheek. "Wake up, Mr Brand. Please. I don't know what to do. I've looked everywhere."

With a sigh of resignation, Stephen opened his lids and stared straight into the blinding blue eyes hovering above him.

"Don't sound so worried, Rosie." He gave her a lazy smile, then did a double-take and sat up hurriedly in the deckchair, frowning at the apparition before him. Red hair – which would have been quite lovely had it been clean and combed – hanging free and falling to the waist; a small, pointed, vivacious face, set atop some kind of trailing medieval gown in creased green satin and silver lace. The wide sleeves were already showing tatters.

"Rosalind Taggard. Why are you still wearing your pageant costume?"

"I thought we'd finished with all that, yesterday ... It doesn't matter, does it?" the child asked in an anxious tone.

"I don't suppose so. Miss Hunter made the dresses: I'm sure she won't mind if you keep yours."

"Oh, it's *hers*, is it?" A quick scowl masked the vivid face.

"I don't think I'll wear it after all. You can give it back to her." The child began to unfasten the laces on the bodice, then hesitated, realizing that she had nothing but her underwear to replace it.

"So," said Stephen placidly, smiling at her predicament, "what are you going to do, little Rosie, parade around in your drawers?"

The hands ceased their fiddling with the fastenings, and the red head snapped up.

"Anyhow," went on Stephen, unperturbed, "you look" – he caught the full effect of the brilliant blue eyes, and finished weakly – "beautiful. But it's hardly the sort of gear for searching out young Dixon, do you think?"

Rosalind's breath went out in a sigh.

"Then you'll help me look for him, Mr Brand?"

"I'd rather not," he drawled. His voice was pleasant, deep, with an easy, humorous undercurrent to it. "But doubtless I will, seeing that I'm expected to show kindness to little children ... Now, are you going to change?"

Rosaling glanced down at her finery.

"I can put my shorts on, if you like?"

"I like."

She moved away from him, her gown trailing the gravel as she headed for the hole in the fence through which she had come. From where he sat, Stephen could see the mounds of rusty tins, the junk and jumble and mess of peelings, paper, and plastic bags which formed the landscaping in the back garden of the cottage next door – the stronghold of the Taggards, where the head of the household dismembered old cars. A ramshackle shed patched together from planks and corrugated iron hid the view of the rear door.

The Taggards were quite the filthiest family Stephen had ever encountered, and it was his misfortune that, in the whole of that beautiful county, they were fated to be his next door neighbours. Most small villages have at least one such family and, feckless, shiftless, and altered neither by help' nor by example, the Taggards had become the inflicted cross of Ardinford.

Rosalind was back within five minutes, in a torn tee-shirt and rolled-up shorts of indeterminate colour and size. Over her shoulder she carried a grubby tapestry bag.

"Well done, sweet Rosie. Now, where shall we start?" mumbled Stephen, still glued fast to his deckchair. The afternoon was warm, and he was tired, and he had no inclination whatsoever to go scouring the countryside for Dixon Taggard. He yawned. "Where have you been, and whom have you asked?"

"Everywhere and everyone," replied Rosalind, with promptness, if not with truth. "And no one has seen him."

"For which, I imagine, they're devoutly grateful."

"I'm sorry, Mr Brand," said Rosalind, standing on one leg. "I know he's a very naughty little boy—"

"The understatement of the year."

"I'm sorry he mucked up your Robin Hood scene, Mr Brand—"

"So am I. And he not only mucked it up, as you put it so colourfully, but he turned the whole thing into a ruddy fiasco. I might — I just might — find the grace to laugh about it in my old age, but Mr Chapworth certainly will not. Mr Chapworth was very, very angry."

Eric Chapworth was the headmaster, and devoid of any sense of humour.

"I'm sorry, Mr Brand."

Stephen sighed. "Stop saying you're sorry, Rosie dear. I'm not blaming you for the little perisher's faults. But I'm thinking how noble I am — or how foolhardy! — to be contemplating inflicting him once more on society."

Rosalind said nothing, merely stood waiting patiently while he levered himself from his chair.

He rose to his feet, a slender, loose-limbed young man with sleepy grey eyes and an indolent manner that belied his mental alertness. Removing a ladybird from his sleeve, he placed the tiny insect carefully in a half-cupped marigold.

"OK Rosie, prime the pump. When did you last see the demon Dixon?"

"Just after the pageant." A curve of smile. "After Mr Chapworth shouted at him, Dix went to the pond to dig out some more wet clay for his animals."

Stephen allowed this incomprehensible explanation to slide. He was looking at Rosalind in dismay, no longer relaxed or disinterested.

"After the pageant! But that was yesterday."

"Yes."

"You haven't seen him since yesterday?"

She shook her head.

Stephen grabbed her arm. "Do you mean to tell me that your brother has been missing all night? Why on earth didn't you say so?"

"I did, or I tried to. It's all right, Mr Brand," soothed Rosalind. "Dix often stays out all night, he's not afraid. He likes sleeping outside."

"What are your parents doing? Aren't they worried?"

"No."

No, they wouldn't be, thought Stephen bitterly. Nothing as basic as a missing child would upset the Taggards. Part tinker, they had alighted in Ardinford by way of Welfare while the eldest son, Joseph, served a term in Medstone jail. Ellery Sugden, of Sugden Court, who owned the pair of remote ex-farm-labourers' cottages, and most of the land around, had benevolently – and misguidedly, Stephen felt – offered the empty dwelling for the relief of the Taggard family. It had been a source of regret to the village ever since.

"What does your father say?" demanded Stephen again.

"He says Dix'll get a good hiding when he comes home," replied Rosalind.

Stephen thought wryly that that just about summed up

the Taggards' care of their children: go where you like, do
what you like, and pay later.

"Then I suppose we'd better contact Sergeant Leach,"
said Stephen resignedly, kissing goodbye to his peaceful
afternoon. "He won't be any too pleased."

"No!" Rosalind looked at him in fright. "Oh, no, Mr
Brand. Please, Mr Brand. My dad'll half kill me if he thinks
I've sent the police round."

That, thought Stephen, having seen the heavy leather
belt in operation, was only too possible. He wondered what
Taggard senior had been up to this time. A lay-about by
nature and a thief by inclination, Digger Taggard set his
family an example they seemed more than willing to
follow. In an earlier age they would have spent their days
travelling from village to village, mending pots and pans
and living off the countryside, part of the scheme of things;
but now, forced to conform, grounded, they were an irritant
to a well-heeled society, which watched with disgust as they
led the marauding life of the dispossessed.

"Rosie —" began Stephen, and broke off helplessly. She
was shaking.

But the boy had already been absent for close on twenty-
four hours: someone in authority should be told.

"Dix has been out all night. He's only a little boy,"
Stephen started again, attempting to be censorious and
failing miserably. He could not imagine anything
disastrous happening to Dix. In his experience, it was not
children like Dixon Taggard, little animals left to fend for
themselves, who came to harm, but the carefully cossetted,
well-protected ones who were rarely allowed out of their
parents' sight.

"I thought you'd help me look for him," went on
Rosalind, in an aggrieved tone. "I've been all over, myself,
but I couldn't find him. I was sure you'd help me if I
asked." Obviously, she thought he was letting the side
down.

With reluctance, Stephen agreed to go with her. In spite

of the fact that the child had been missing for nearly a night and a day, his overriding feeling was one of irritation rather than concern.

"Not to the police," insisted Rosalind. "You won't tell the police? My dad'll kill you."

"I doubt that," said Stephen, his voice dry. "I doubt that very much." He could have offered to take on Digger Taggard single-handed, but he knew his capabilities. "Anyhow, your brother can hardly be left wandering around on his own, he may be hurt ..."

"Not the police," repeated Rosalind stubbornly.

They went on in much the same vein for several minutes, with Stephen patently getting nowhere. Then he said, capitulating: "OK Rosalind. I'll compromise ... Do you know what a compromise is, Rosie?"

"No."

"Well, it means that I'm prepared to meet you halfway ... I'll give you a couple of hours of my valuable time. and if we've not turned him up by then, we see Sergeant Leach, whether your father likes it or not."

Rosalind squirmed rebelliously.

Looking in the direction of the Taggards' cottage, Stephen said: "I suppose I'd better have a word with your father." He kicked aside a pile of fletched arrows which he had been detailed to return to the rectory, where most of the props for the various plays and village fêtes were always stored, and made for the adjoining fence.

"I shouldn't," warned Rosalind.

Stephen halted, and stared back at her.

"He's drunk and as mad as a hatter in there. He'll only sling you out on your ear."

Stephen was no coward, but he was no half-blinkered hero, either: he knew his limitations. And burly Digger Taggard, who could crack a nut with his fist and a head with a single blow in one of his drunken rages, was one of them. Stephen remembered his last confrontation with the man, and his throat burned at the memory. No matter that the accusations had been untrue, the taste was still there, in his mouth. Acrid, bile. No, Stephen had no wish to tangle with Digger Taggard, who had a mind like a cesspit and attributed his own base motives to everyone else. Digger Taggard, who was strong as a bull and who had never done an honest stroke of work, and certainly never touched a shovel, in his life.

Stephen retreated. "And you say that you've asked around the village?"

Rosalind nodded. "Nobody's seen Dix since the pageant, yesterday. They all remembered him there."

They would, thought Stephen bitterly.

"It was a lovely pageant, wasn't it?" smiled Rosalind, looking up at him with shining eyes. Even Dixon had not managed to spoil the day for her. "And the rector promised that we could have any of the throwaway stuff we wanted, if we went to the pavilion this morning."

"Well, then, have you tried there? Dix is probably scavenging." The Taggards were notorious scavengers. Rosalind said she had, and everywhere else where her young brother might have been expected to go.

Her eyes had clouded once more. "That's why I can't understand Dix being away for so long. I know he's often very naughty, and I know he wanders off and sometimes hides from me, but he wanted to collect the things that were left over. We had made plans to take carrier-bags and clear the lot. Besides –" She broke off, scowling.

"Well?"

"I was helping him with his zoo. That was what he was keen on at the moment. He's made all these clay animals, see, and I'd said I'd build the cages for him. We'd got these cardboard boxes, and sticks, and –"

"I expect something else caught his attention, and he forgot. Don't worry, Rosalind. He can't be far off. You know what he's like. This won't be the first time he's gone missing." Nor the second, nor the third, he thought grimly.

Searching for young Dix was becoming one of the certainties in life. Even then, with all the warnings staring him in the face, Stephen remained unconcerned about the boy's fate. The child was a nuisance, nothing more.

Idly, he wondered if he could enlist Alison, his fiancée, in this unwelcome exercise. She was the class teacher for the six-year-olds in the local school, and had the dubious privilege, five days a week, heaven help her, of imparting the three Rs to Dixon Taggard. But she would be teaching in Sunday School at this moment, and later was pledged to play the organ for evening service, owing to the default of the regular organist – George Flowerdew was a devout member of the rector's flock, but given to fits of temperament and even out-and-out rebellion, and this, evidently, was one of those time – As the rector's daughter, Alison was, even more than Stephen, it seemed, at the village's beck and call. And she, too, had borne a great deal of the brunt of the pageant. In fairness, Stephen rejected the possibility of Alison's help.

"And you've no idea why your brother might have gone off? Apart from yesterday's little bag of tricks, he's not been in trouble with anyone else, has he?"

Rosalind's eyes flickered, but she merely said: "No, Mr Brand."

"Come on, then," he said, turning. "We'd better make some kind of start."

"You're not goin' to the rectory, are you?" asked Rosalind suspiciously.

"No." Stephen looked at her. "Miss Hunter will be busy this afternoon."

"That's all right then, only I don't want her poking her nose in."

"That's not a very nice thing to say."

"She don't like me."

"Perhaps she doesn't find you very likable." Rosalind, with her fierce loves and quick hates, her devastating tongue, and her fine imitation of a prickly pear.

"No more does she like Dix very much, and he gave her a frog. His best one, and all."

"Maybe Miss Hunter isn't too keen on frogs."

"A *clay* frog," Rosalind explained with patience. "I mean one made with clay … He made this." She pulled a small horse from her tapestry bag. It was crudely but vigorously executed, in raw, red clay, with a mane of teased string and eyes of thick, opaque glass.

"That's the last thing he made. Yesterday. Before the pageant," said Rosalind. "It's good, ain't it?"

Stephen agreed that it was. Very good. The clay must have come from the diggings of the new drainage system beside the old pound, near the village pond. The horse's eyes appeared to be made from fragments of a heavy, broken glass, and he could guess where that had come from, also. He recalled a day, more than a week ago, when old Pott's ancient Ford had rattled round the corner far too fast and been clipped by the baker's van. Dixon Taggard had been there, sweeping up the small squares of glass from the shattered windscreen, and scooping them into a plastic bag – everything was grist to the Taggard mill.

He watched Rosalind slip the horse back into her shoulder-bag, then he touched her arm.

"We'll begin in the village, someone may have seen him recently."

"No, they ain't," contradicted the child at his side. But she smiled at him in relief, the cares of the day falling from her shoulders, and he reflected that it was so easy to win a child's trust, even a child from a family as suspicious and anti-social as the Taggards.

To be fair, Rosalind was the best of the bunch, and a pretty good best, at that. It was not that she was so much cleaner or more honest, but rather an innate clarity of spirit which singled her out from the rest. She was bright, interested, and, at the moment, worshipping at Stephen's feet. He admitted to himself more than a little care for

Rosalind; he had gone out of his way, many times, to help her, both in and out of school, and she had responded. He felt a glow of pride in his achievement. Nearly a year in his class and care had turned her from a surly, back-biting little misfit, into an outgoing, sensible eleven-year-old.

Except that Rosalind would never be like the average eleven-year-old ... Life had etched far more than the fair span of years on her yardstick, had made her more knowledgeable and, at the same time, perhaps, more vulnerable. She no longer had a child's protective innocence.

Alison had warned him to take care, that being Rosalind's teacher was one thing, being Rosalind's great and golden idol was quite another. "The child is more than a little in love with you," Alison had said in her cool, pleasant voice.

He had refuted the idea, while knowing it to be fact. But how, with a child, and a child who had known as little care and affection as Rosalind, did one unbind the – figuratively – clinging hands? He did not know, and it would have taken a much crueller nature than Stephen's to have tried. He knew what it was like to be the outsider, to be the one with no one to love, no one to care for. Perhaps that had been the magnet, the call of like to like, for his own early life had been nothing to sing praises about.

Not that his problem had been a too-prolific family, more the lack of one. He had been brought up in a children's home, belonging to no one and hailing, so it appeared, from nowhere, and though his easy-going nature had seen to it that his passage had been a reasonably tranquil one, he had been left with the envy of the institutionalised for those with established family-based lives, and with an abiding desire to dig in some roots for himself.

When, at the age of twelve, his coach had halted in Ardinford during a day's outing to some coastal resort or other, he had fallen in love with the place, with its beautiful cluster of ancient tiled roofs, its bright river curling slowly through grassy, flower-dotted fields, its dim woods and sleeping trees and wholly enchanted air of having stepped outside both space and time. And then and there, standing on the Green with the sun on his head and a sheet of daisies at his feet, he had promised himself that, one day, he would be a part of everything he saw.

With a tenacity unusual in him, Stephen had worked and schemed his way to his goal. Now, a few years out of teachers' training college, he was in charge of the oldest children in Ardinford's primary school, and well on his way to establishing his chosen niche. It was only recently, coming into contact with the Taggards, that Stephen had been forced to question whether there might not be, perhaps, children worse off in their own homes, with their own families, than he, in his impersonal children's home, had ever been.

Maybe, after all, his aching sense of deprivation was not particularly necessary.

Ardinford was the kind of little, lost, dreaming place where nothing of more than parochial interest ever happened, and where the industrial revolution had been resisted to the last ditch and broken ploughshare. Yet even there, it seemed, violent events must occasionally have impinged on the tranquillity – as witnessed the village war memorial, grey granite on a humpbacked hillock of green, with its double column of names, more than a handspan long, the flower of Ardinford's young men. "They Shall Live For Evermore." But forgotten now, except in a token service one day a year, with two minutes silence lost in the hum of non-ceasing activity, and the foot of the memorial-stone overgrown with quaking-grass and a patriotic confusion of snowy daisies, heavenly blue clary, and the bold, blood-scarlet of poppies.

The poppies were early this year. Not yet late June and the banks everywhere were ablaze with them, called out by the recent long spell of hot weather. The grass, too, was ready for cutting. In the distance, from the south, there came the sound of gunshots: someone was probably after pigeons in the woods.

Stephen followed Rosalind's long brown legs through the gate on to the rough track that led along the back of the cottage gardens. Unfenced and wild, the path snaked downwards across rough farmland and the Sugden property, skirting the old chalk quarry, in a lonely, flower-scented short cut to the village.

The cottages were isolated, the lane that passed their doors rarely travelled except for an occasional farm truck or a member of the Taggard tribe on a decrepit bicycle; and even fewer were the people who used the short cut, so that, at this time of year, with nature at her most abundant, it was almost impossible to beat one's way through the tangle of bush and bramble on either side without the aid of a flame-thrower or a machete. Further along, where a network of other paths from various outflung farms joined and criss-crossed, the going became fairly reasonable – a padded, pollen-scattered way of ripened grasses, buttercup, sorrel, and wide-lashed ox-eye daisies.

Mrs Taggard was in her back garden, as they went past, with a couple of pre-school Taggards. Even now, in the hot sunshine, the children had that running nosed, pinched look of the neglected poor. Since Welfare, their lot had no doubt improved on that of their ancestors, but, then, so had the ability of Father Taggard to pay for drinks and dogs. It was a vicious, ravelled coil, and one, it seemed, impossible to unknot.

"Good afternoon, Mrs Taggard," called Stephen, in greeting.

She lifted a flat, closed face, and nodded at him.

"I hear young Dixon's missing again," said Stephen.

Once more she nodded. "Rosie was supposed to be lookin' after him, weren't she?" She picked up a filthy dummy from the path at her feet, wiped it perfunctorily on her skirt, and thrust it into the drooling mouth of the baby astride her hip.

"It might be better," Stephen said mildly, "if you left less of the child-minding to Rosalind."

The flat face stared back at him, "I dunno what yer mean."

"Oh, I'm sure you do, Mrs Taggard."

At that point, Digger Taggard himself shambled into the doorway, rheumy-eyed and with three days' growth of beard. He slouched against the doorpost.

"Clear off," he shouted, hawking spittle over the step, "and mind yer own business ... And keep yer 'ands off our Rosie –" He made a threatening lunge forward and trod on the fingers of the child crawling near his feet. The injured party promptly set up a thin wailing.

Turning away quickly, Stephen unhooked a bramble from his trouser-leg and followed in the tracks of Rosalind who had already disappeared along the path.

Two

"Look out, here comes old Henny-Penny," hissed Rosalind, some twenty minutes later, as they vaulted the stile which brought them out on to the tree-lined lane that led into the village. "Don't let her grab us."

Stephen stared at her with his brows up, until Rosalind amended hastily, turning pink: "Miss James, I mean."

"I should think so. And don't be so ruthless with your adjectives. Miss James isn't so many years older than I am." Not for the first time, as he contemplated the fussy little woman fast bearing down on them, he thought how cruel children were, and how devastatingly accurate. Poor Miss James who in her late-twenties already bore the ingrained marks of middle-age. Gushing, garrulous, kind, with her finger in every village pie, she was given a wide berth by the children, large and small alike, and was deeply hurt that her effusive overtures were met with stony silence – and sometimes worse. Today, her round face was peony-red from the heat.

"Whew, Stephen, isn't it a scorcher?" she greeted him. Then she turned to the girl. "Hello, Rosalind – I'm just taking some lettuces to your mother."

"We don't like lettuce," growled Rosalind, ungraciously.

Stephen gave her a little dig with his elbow but failed to prod her into any sign of appreciation.

"They're beauties," he said, peering into the carrier-bag. "Good solid hearts."

Miss James looked pleased. "I'll leave a couple on your doorstep."

"That's very kind of you." It was useless to resist. Miss James never took "no" for an answer, and produced vast quantities of organically-grown vegetables which she distributed like largesse around the village.

She was staring at them inquisitively. "Where are you both off to?"

"Dix Taggard is missing again," said Stephen.

"That doesn't surprise me," observed Miss James. "He usually is." She smiled at Rosalind. "Don't worry about your little brother, dear."

"I'm not," said Rosalind hardily.

"That's right, dear. He's bound to turn up. Like a bad penny." She tittered. "He really is a naughty little boy, isn't he? I thought I should die when I saw all those apple cores at the pageant yesterday. The grand finale! Robin Hood out of William Tell! And all those boy archers ready to dazzle us with their skill ... I imagine, by sleight of hand, they were supposed to impale their apples with the arrows before holding them up for us to see?" She suddenly dissolved into helpless giggles once more. "... If only they had had the presence of mind not to flourish the cores on the tips of their shafts –"

"Yes," said Stephen.

Rosalind stared at her balefully.

"Oh, I'm sorry," spluttered Miss James. "I shouldn't laugh, should I? It had taken you so long to arrange ... And then the bob-apples, too, at the side-show afterwards, all cores –" She stifled her mirth, and wagged her head. "Naughty little boy. Perhaps that's why he's run off. Maybe he was afraid of what people would say."

Rosalind switched at the swaying daisies with her shoulder-bag. "Oh, no," she said, regarding Miss James from under her lashes. "He didn't care about *that*. He didn't care about that at all."

No, thought Stephen, hiding a grin. Dix wouldn't. A Taggard wouldn't care about something as trivial as wrecking a term's work.

He said: "I suppose you haven't seen him, today?"

Miss James considered. "He was sitting on the bank beside Cynthia Chubb's cottage this morning ... Oh, no –" She corrected herself. "That was yesterday morning, of course, the morning of the pageant. He was playing there, then, with a bag of some kind."

Rosalind made a sharp little movement.

"Almost everybody saw him after that," she said in exasperation.

"I'm sorry, I'm sure," bridled Miss James. "We can't all have perfect memories."

"Well, thank you, anyhow," smiled Stephen, pouring oil. "And now we'd better be on our way –" He grasped Rosalind's elbow.

"Stupid cow," muttered the child, as Miss James fluttered her fingers at them and trotted off along the lane in the direction of the Taggards' cottage.

"She means well," remonstrated Stephen.

Rosalind uttered a non-committal noise, then said: "I'd sooner have Miss Hunter than her, at least Miss Hunter isn't always going around doing good."

"Than which, nothing greater can be said," returned Stephen dryly.

"Oh, I know she's your fancy, and all that –"

"– And all that," he agreed.

Rosalind giggled. "Sorry, Mr Brand."

"And so you should be." But it was true, he thought. Rosalind had flicked a raw nerve there. Roped into everything that was going, Alison remained, nevertheless, detached. She had the habit of isolating herself in space. Yet perhaps that was the consequence of her upbringing, as his concern for stability and roots was the result of his.

A child of privilege, the offspring of the rector of this parish, who with a considerable private income of his own had been able to make sure that his only child was hedged around from care, Alison had always been Queen Bee. A private school, a generous allowance – that she had trained to teach was some personal, peculiar battle for independence of her own, but, even there, she had been a day student, unsullied by the hurly-burly of communal existence.

All her life had been spent in Ardinford rectory, the lovely old house dating back three hundred years or more, whose chimneys could just be seen through the horse-chestnut trees on the far side of the Green. Outside, ancient, tranquil, untouched by time: inside, beautiful. Panelled wainscoting, handsome furniture, luxurious appointments. Stephen knew little about the good things of life, but even he was able to recognize that everything in the Hunters' home was exquisite.

He thought wryly: Alison, let me take you away from all this —

Still, things could hardly have been easy for her, entrusted with the running of that huge old rectory after her mother died when Alison was barely into her teens. Granted, Mary Witherspoon helped to look after the place, but the main responsibility rested on Alison's fragile shoulders. Though she tackled that, as she did everything else, with calm efficiency.

Alison had been born with the power of managing recalcitrant parishioners, difficult old gentlemen, mad dogs, and little children, and did it without any apparent effort. Oddly enough, while distrusting the benevolent Miss James, the small fry found Alison more than satisfactory: she listened to them, taught them, and dispensed even-handed, unsympathetic justice. They asked no more.

But was that enough for him? Stephen kicked aside a stone.

Really, he was fortunate to have won her, although, to be honest, he could never remember actually proposing. More a hint here and there, and Alison had organized everything else, with her cool little smile. Stephen wondered what her father had thought about it all. It did not strike him that the rector was altogether pleased with his prospective son-in-law. No doubt Hunter would have preferred the *status quo*. But, then, maybe that would have been the case whomsoever Alison had chosen.

It was a sensible match on Stephen's side: the rector's daughter was the catch of the season in Ardinford, but sometimes Stephen wondered if he had not, perhaps, taken her as an easy way into the community. She, and her father, her friends, and her home, represented what he had so long been denied, people and a place of his own. With her beside him, he would be fully accepted into the life of the village. He would belong. But was he really using her, quite cold-bloodedly, to further his own ends?

For a moment, he scowled. No one could call it a passionate relationship. If Alison did not hold him at arm's length, she certainly did not encourage any little intimacies. A chaste kiss now and then was the most she had offered. Once, he had tried to overcome her reserve, had taken her in his arms and kissed her violently, feeling the fire in his own body responding to the closeness of hers. But she had extricated herself neatly, and with that same cool little smile which sometimes so deflated him. And he had not pursued the matter. So perhaps the fault, after all, lay in himself, for he was a man not unduly troubled by sexual fancies. Oh, the occasional erotic dream and wish-fulfillment waking thought of naked flesh to flesh; of Eve unclothed. But little more.

He was not a vain man. He had no idea what qualities Alison could have seen in him to choose to link her life with his. He was not particularly good-looking, though he did have the clear-cut almost boyish features which might have some appeal. Apart from that, he was healthy, of medium height and lightly built, with straight fair hair bleached fairer by the sun, eyes of a clear grey traced with charcoal, like flecks of shade on sunlit water, and the kind of easy-going nature which some people found infuriating. That he was kind and generous, gentle, even, never occurred to him.

Anyhow, Alison's environment, it seemed, had not been

one where demonstrative affection was encouraged. He had never seen the rector kiss or caress his daughter, although Stephen was well aware that the man loved her. But loved her as he would a possession? A valued treasure? A piece of cherished porcelain? This is mine – keep off? Stephen did not know, and was not equipped to guess. He himself had been brought up in circumstances where physical contact was kept to a minimum. He knew only that something was missing from his relationship with Alison. Perhaps, when they were married ...

"There's Miss Chubb," grimaced Rosalind. "You gonna ask her about Dix?"

Cynthia Chubb's small cottage was situated by itself beside the war memorial, which they were passing now on its grassy bank, where it stood knee-deep in summer flowers. Stephen could see marguerites blossoming through the school-children's November wreath of fading plastic poppies.

Miss Chubb was at her gate, just about to wheel her bicycle through into the road, and wearing her habitual scatty air of a harassed haystack. Her bicycle-basket was full of leaflets. Her hat was askew.

"She's nutty," proclaimed Rosalind, sotto-voce.

"Hearing your comments on the good persons in this village is an education in itself," murmured Stephen. "You might be within your rights to call her slightly unusual, but decidely not nutty."

"– as a fruitcake," insisted Rosalind.

Miss Chubb rolled her eyes when they approached her, and denied all knowledge of the whereabouts of Dixon Taggard, yesterday, today, or any other day, and realizing that any further pressure would have reduced her to a state of gibbering incoherence, Stephen stood aside and waited while she hauled her square figure on to her bicycle. Everything about Miss Chubb was square, from the square-cut bob of her hair, down to the square-toed brogues on her feet. Even her glasses had sturdy square rims. They, too, were askew. He watched her gather herself together and pedal off furiously in the direction of the open countryside, where she was to be found most days, collecting plants and berries in season, and queer fungi which she claimed were edible and presumably were as it was evident she had not succumbed to them.

"Nutty!" said Rosalind in disgust, surveying the retreating back.

"Every village is entitled to its one eccentric."

"Is that what she is?" Rosalind looked after Miss Chubb with interest. "I thought she was a child murderess. Somebody told me so."

"Then somebody should be locked up." Stephen frowned at her. "You'll get into trouble if you run around saying such terrible things."

"You don't think –" began Rosalind, rounding her eyes and drawing in her breath, "that she could have taken –?"

"No," cut in Stephen. "Certainly not. She'd never put a hand on Dix, or anyone else, for that matter. Whatever she did was nothing like that. And stop gossiping Rosie Taggard, or the next time I take you swimming I might be tempted to try a little child suppression myself, and hold you under."

Rosalind giggled. "That'd be the day! You know I can outswim and outbreathe you any day, Mr Brand."

"My excellent tuition."

"My excellent legs and lungs, more like." Rosalind returned to the topic of most interest. "Anyhow, I heard that Miss Chubb had murdered a couple of kids, oh, a long time ago, and –"

"Where do you children pick up your ideas?"

"It's true."

Stephen sighed. "All right, then. But not in the way you're telling it," he reproved. "Miss Chubb, when she was very, very young, and with no one to give her any advice, failed to look after some children in her care properly, that's all."

"They died?"

"They died. She loved them, but they died. It was sad, and perhaps avoidable if people had understood what was going on. But it was not murder. Neglect, maybe, but not murder. She just did not know how to cope—"

"She was put away, though, wasn't she?" replied Rosalind, with the harsh logic of a child.

"For a time."

"And it was Mr Hunter who salvaged her?"

"Rehabilitated might be a better choice of word, said Stephen, and laughed down at her with his eyes. "Yes. I believe it was. She lives in one of his cottages now, anyway."

"I suppose rectors have to be nice to people. It's their job, really, isn't it? Funny, though ..."

"How so?"

"About Mr Hunter. He's not like that, is he?"

Stephen raised his brows in query.

"Well," pursued Rosalind, struggling, "if I were in trouble, I wouldn't go to Mr Hunter. Not at any price. I'd go to you. Or I might go to Mr Flowerdew, or Mrs Witherspoon, at a pinch. But not Mr Hunter." She paused. "He ... looks through you."

Stephen knew exactly what she meant, and pondered the enigma that was his future father-in-law. Hunter was of a strange, implacable nature; still; guarded; not given to easy relationships. And yet he accorded well enough with his parishioners. They, it seemed, found something in their rector that was denied to Stephen, who had the feeling that Hunter did indeed look through him, and was not altogether impressed by what he saw.

Stephen glanced down the row of neat cottages on the left hand side of the road. Miss Chubb's, tiny and squarely-built like its tenant, facing the Green and the village pond, where May-flies were dancing in the heat, then a row of five more cottages, all immaculate, with gleaming windows and spruce white fences, standing in bee-haunted, well-tended gardens. the scent of roses hung heavy on the air. These cottages were all owned by the rector, who kept a hawk's eye on paintwork and general presentation. Not a weed flourished there but that was noted and duly condemned.

Pretty places they were, adding to the picture-postcard effect of this end of the village, and had featured on calendars and cracker-boxes, Stephen had heard. Well, good for them, he told himself, but he was unworthily pleased to see that a non-conformist had sprung up in their midst. George Flowerdew, one time bellringer and present organist – when it suited him, which at this moment it did not – was applying a second coat of canary-yellow paint to his front door. The colour sang out, a piercing, too-bright note among the soft greens and gentle browns of its neighbours, and was the cause of the present estrangement with the rector. While perversely remaining on the side of Flowerdew, Stephen could see exactly why Hunter disliked the innovation. Wryly, he wondered how long the old man would be able to hold out. Doubtless, the big guns would be going in soon, for few defied Kelvin Hunter, and none with any permanence.

Stephen himself invariably came off second best in any altercation with his future father-in-law. The trouble was – he smiled crookedly to himself – he rarely sensed when they were riding into battle, and he had been unhorsed, unhelmed, disarmed, before he had been made aware of any necessity for fight.

He stared around. The village street and the Green seemed curiously bereft of the younger element. They couldn't all be in Sunday School, surely?

"Where have all the children gone?" he demanded of Rosalind.

"Captain Sugden's allowing us to use his swimming pool for the summer, free of charge. Everybody's there."

"Oh, yes, I'd forgotten."

"He's going to open Sugden Court to the public next year, and he's having new car parks and roads and things built. Only then, of course, it will cost money to go in." She gave him a quick, lovely smile. "You see, when he dies, there'll be no one to inherit the place, so I suppose the public is the next best thing."

"Aren't you writing off Captain Sugden's chances rather soon? The poor man's not yet forty." Stephen's tone was amused. "He has plenty of time to get himself a wife and a dozen offspring, if he chooses."

"Oh, no, he can't. Because of his accident —"

"And who told you that?" asked Stephen.

"Oh, everyone knows that," said Rosalind airily.

It was true that the village liked to know all that one did, and why one did it. Once, the Reverend Kelvin Hunter had said as much to Stephen, warning him that life in Ardinford had to be lived as if it were an open book. It was only when people thought they knew all that there was to know about you, that you could rest in peace. Well, Hunter's life was certainly open enough: people were in and out of the rectory all day long. Stephen was not sure that he wanted to live his days on quite such an exposed plane. A vague memory stirred in his mind. Someone, somewhere, a very long time ago, had remarked that openness was also the most effective camouflage there was.

He turned again to Rosalind. "Maybe Dix is at the pool."

"No, I checked. And Captain Sugden said he'd take his Land-Rover and patrol the estate, and ask his work-gang to keep an eye open. But that was this morning, so Dix couldn't have been anywhere there, or he'd have been brought back by now, wouldn't he?"

Stephen had to admit the logic of her argument.

Three

"Afternoon, Brand," called Chapworth, the headmaster, from his gate as they went past. "Have you seen Alison today?"

"No," replied Stephen.

"Pity. I was wondering how much we'd made out of yesterday's pageant. She's totalling the profits from the various stalls and side-shows."

Oh, thought Stephen, so they'd put that on Alison, too. It was certainly no picnic being the rector's daughter. But no doubt she'd cope with that, as she did with everything else, in her usual efficient fashion.

Chapworth bent towards Rosalind. "And what are you doing, young Rosie? Why aren't you splashing around with the rest?"

Rosalind was forced to repeat her tale of woe.

"What do you mean, girl, you can't find your brother?"

Haltingly, Rosalind replied that what she honestly meant was that she couldn't find her brother.

"Hmmph," grunted Chapworth, when the saga ended. "And where are you off to now?"

Stephen explained that he and Rosalind were checking Dixon's known haunts, and inquiring whether anyone had seen the child that day. They intended to stop at the post office, and then try the disused railway station where the village children often played.

After a further word or two with Stephen, the

headmaster offered to round up some help and scour the countryside towards Redeham.

"Thanks," said Stephen, relieved that the affair no longer rested entirely on his shoulders.

"All in the cause of duty," said Chapworth. His brows lowered for a moment. "I'd like a word with young Dixon myself, about the missing bran-tub novelties. My wife insists that the child had them stuffed inside his shirt." A sudden point occurred to him. "No car, today, Brand?"

"No," replied Stephen. "It's still at the garage ... It's been promised to me by tomorrow, though. I've said I'd take Alison into Redeham on Tuesday, to catch the noon coach. She's going to stay with her cousin Veronica for the rest of the week." He looked glum. Hunter usually managed to ensure that Alison was able to spend as little time as possible with her fiancé.

"With Veronica? Alison is going to Veronica's?" Chapworth sounded surprised. "I shouldn't think the rector is very pleased about that."

"On the contrary. He arranged it." Stephen's mouth quirked. "Probably aiming to forestall any evil designs I might have on his daughter ... lusts of the flesh called out by the sun and a week's leisure —"

Chapworth said: "Do you mean to tell me that our Reverend is acknowledging Veronica's existence?" He looked unconvinced. "She used to live with the Hunters, you know, after Alison's mother died. There was an almighty row a few years back — something to do with Ellery Sugden, I believe. The Captain was quite keen on Alison at one time, before he tripped that bomb in Ireland, poor devil — not that she ever gave him any encouragement. Real cool she was. But Veronica would have been very pleased to see her cousin mistress of Sugden Court, only Hunter wasn't having any of it."

"Water under the bridge," said Stephen.

There it was again, he thought. Gossip. They all indulged in it as a regular pastime, every man-Jack of them. One man's business was every man's business, and he hadn't grown used to it yet, for all that he'd been among them for so many months. He wondered what on earth the village had done for its diversion during the last war, when the army had occupied Sugden Court and dumped an ammunition store in the old chalk quarry – and posters had proclaimed on every side that "Careless Talk Costs Lives." He'd take a bet that that little exhortation to seal lips had made small difference in Ardinford, which had probably gossiped its way through every battle from Harold's at Hastings.

"Yes ... Well ..." Chapworth looked at Stephen's face and changed the subject quickly. "Anyhow, I thought you'd like to know that your section of the pageant went very well, Brand." He spoke grudgingly. "The bow and arrow scene was most effective, and it was a stroke of genius to provide archery butts afterwards on the sideshows. They were very popular ... Pity young Taggard had to spike your finale, I suppose."

Stephen ignored the commiseration. He was sick to death of the pageant.

"Don't let young Dixon worry you," went on Chapworth, his eyes following Rosalind as she scuffed away from them down the street. "He goes missing with the regularity of an unfettered hound. He's used to living rough and sleeping under the stars. It's the tinker blood in him, and it's something no one will eradicate. Unfortunately, it falls on the village to turn out and find him."

Today, however, the village was not turning out; the village was exhausted by its communal efforts of the day before. Stephen regarded the supine forms in the deckchairs in the various gardens around him. No one had seen the child. And no one, apparently, cared.

The consensus of opinion was that Dix would roll up – eventually.

"There were strangers in the village yesterday," remarked Stephen. "In to see the pageant."

"Oh, most of them were relations of some sort or other, or friends from the neighbouring villages. No one in their right mind would touch Dixon Taggard with a barge-pole ... He'll come home, right enough, wagging his tail behind him. He always does," said Chapworth. "Enjoy your half-term, you need it after the work that went into yesterday's performance – although a week's break is far too long, the children will be as wild as werewolves by the time they return to school."

"Oh, I shouldn't think so."

"No? Well, you'll have to slick them back into shape," said the headmaster, lugubriously. "It's the swimming gala next, isn't it? I can't say I believe you're doing the right thing putting a Taggard in it, even if she can swim like a fish. Odd little devil. She's bound to cause more trouble than she's worth."

Stephen said: "Thanks to her, we're in with a chance for the first time in years."

He swung away from Chapworth and hurried across to where Rosalind's toes were still digging up dirt. Chapworth's voice floated after them.

"– And if you find young Taggard, send him along to me, tell him I'd like a word –"

"That should make sure Dix enjoys his holiday," growled Rosalind.

Stephen shushed her and hustled her forward by the elbow.

"He's potty if he thinks Dix'll come within a mile of him," she said, voicing Stephen's own private opinion. "He shouldn't have put that bran-tub where anybody could get at it." Anybody, meaning Dixon Taggard.

Suddenly she gave a joyful little skip. "Oh, there's Rich," she cried, and hurtled towards a dark-haired youth who was striding along the road towards them, a shotgun under his arm, and a brace of rabbits in his hand. For all he lacked the foxy mane of Rosalind, he was most obviously a Taggard – the same pointed cast of countenance, the same unwavering, deep blue eyes, the same bony, under-nourished frame.

"You catch those?" she panted, drawing level.

"Who else? ... Take your bloody paws off." This to his sister who was stroking the soft, speckled grey fur. He turned his head. "Afternoon, Mr Brand."

"Good afternoon, Richlyn. Been poaching?"

"No." The thin shoulders hunched defensively. "Captain Sugden's given us permission to shoot his south wood." A token gesture, Stephen guessed, as the Taggards would have helped themselves anyway, but doubtless Sugden hoped it might serve to keep them away from the north where he had young stock.

Stephen grinned. "I was only joking, Richlyn. The farmers'll be only too pleased if you keep the rabbits down, and the pigeons, too, if you're any great shot."

"Fair enough."

"I thought I'd heard guns popping off all week."

"Gotta live, and the old man'll do nothing ... Do you know if he's in?"

"He was a short while ago. I suppose you know that Dix is still missing?"

"Damn Dix!" Richlyn Taggard hitched the gun higher under his arm and strode off down the road swinging his rabbits. Rosalind looked after him with admiration.

"He's almost as good a shot as Joseph," she said. Joseph, the eldest and most beloved brother, who was immured in Medstone jail and not due out for another eighteen months – unless fortune smiled.

"Rich!" she screeched after the fast-retreating back. "Can I have a rabbit's foot?"

Her brother chose to ignore the cry and carried on his way.

"They're lucky," said Rosalind briefly, in explanation, turning once more to Stephen. "I'm goin' to carry it in my tee-shirt."

"Good God," ejaculated Stephen, startled.

"I'll ask Rich for one for you, too, if you like?" Rosalind looked thoughtful. "Some people trim them with silver. I haven't got any silver, Mr Brand, but I can wrap a piece of tinfoil round it. Would that do?"

"Admirably, I should think," replied Stephen gravely. "I'll keep it in a jar in my – my workroom."

The long red hair swept against his arm. "Will you? Will you really?"

"Well …" He considered. "Until it goes rotten, or the fur falls out, or something."

"Mr Hunter says charms are all superstitious nonsense."

"Every man to his own creed," returned Stephen, his voice placid. He paused with one hand on the side door of the tiny shop-cum-post office which crouched at the far end of the Green. "Have you asked about Dix in here?"

Rosalind nodded. "Mrs Drummond hasn't seen him since yesterday, when he kicked her cat."

So that was that. No one had seen the child around the village. Or, at least, no one could recall seeing him after about six o'clock the previous evening. Mrs Drummond rang round the nearby farms for them, but drew another blank. And still no one was concerned about the child's disappearance. It had happened too often to be news. And that anything harmful could have befallen him seemed unthinkable: the Taggards of this world bore a charmed life.

For an hour or more, Stephen and Rosalind combed the surrounding woods and meadows where Dix was known to play, and, shouting and hallooing, trod the path beside the shallow river Ardin, which meandered a slow course through the fields and woodlands of Ardinford. But the boy was nowhere there, either, not unless he was deliberately hiding. Neither did he appear to be at the disused railway station, where he and some of the other children had concocted a hideout.

Today, Stephen and Rosalind found the place utterly still; deserted. Only the churring of grasshoppers around them, and the bubbling song of sky-larks high up in the blue over the silent track.

Stephen called. His voice bounced back hollowly from the shell of the station building. The place had been closed for years, and part of the roof had fallen in. A boarded window hung on one hinge. He pulled a broken lath aside and peered in. Nothing. Nothing but dust and torn paper, and last autumn's dried leaves lying in heaps in the freckled sunshine.

Squatting near a clumb of nettles, he ripped away the clinging stems of bindweed and peered beneath the platform, a favourite hiding place for Dix on many occasions. But not today. The sun beat hot on Stephen's neck and shoulders.

Slowly, he straightened, and looked up and down the track, which was overgrown and a confusion of waving grasses and weeds. Untouched by knife or chemical spray, here Nature had reclaimed her own. Sorrel and poppies flushed the banking, barbed tendrils of wild roses formed bridal arches above young hawthorns, and everywhere were the fire-spires of foxgloves and rose-bay willowherb. The rampant brambles were already clawing over the edges of the platform. And everywhere, too, more than he had seen in many summers, were the shifting, kaleidoscopic patterns of butterflies, attracted by the unshorn bounty around them.

Rosalind ceased her shouting and her questing circles, and ran back to Stephen.

"It's very odd," she said.

Stephen had to admit that. It was, to say the least of it, very odd. Dixon Taggard appeared to have vanished from the face of his own childish earth.

"He wouldn't," said Rosalind again, obstinately. "He wouldn't have gone off. He had too many things he wanted to do."

But he had gone, seemingly, and left no trail to follow.

And there was nowhere else to look.

Together, they sat on the bank in the late-afternoon sunshine. The cream-coloured elder flowers above them were in full bloom, giving off their heavy, fruity scent. A few stray petals powdered down across Rosalind's bright sunset hair as she reached up to pick a bloom.

"To guard you against witches," she grinned, pushing the stem into the breast pocket of Stephen's shirt. The thick scent caught at his throat. And the smell of elder flowers was forever afterwards to remind him of Rosalind.

"I suppose we had better make tracks for home," he said, at last. "You know of no other place where your brother might be?"

Rosalind shot him a swift upward glance. "There's the old smoke chimney," she said tentatively. "He sometimes plays there. He's built himself a den."

"Where do you mean?"

"There's an old chimney, up on Brenn hill."

Stephen remembered it. An old smoke outlet standing in isolation on the hill, a relic of the days when steam trains still used the tunnel on the line.

"But that's two miles away. He'd never have gone there … would he?"

"Sometimes."

"Oh, hell!" Stephen took her hand, a thin, brown hand scratched and torn from scrambling around the countryside. "I suppose we'd better go and check. Have you been there today?"

She shook her head.

"Come on then. And if he's not there, then that's it. If he's not at home when we get back, it will have to be the police." And dogs, and small armies of men, and a full scale search, he thought grimly.

"Yes," she said slowly, her eyes reflecting back the summer sky. "Yes."

The ruined chimney, its crumbling brickwork looking for all the world like a decaying tooth, stood stark, black, and silent against the skyline.

Stephen felt his skin prickle.

"You mean, he goes up there?" he demanded in awe, eyeing the raw-edged skeleton above them. Here and there, cancerous patches of lichen showed yellow on the dark brick.

"Yes."

Around the smoke stack grew a few stunted hawthorn trees, their blossoms already rusting into the beginnings of fruit. A young oak pressed in close against the brickwork.

Stephen remained with his head tilted, looking up.

"There." Rosalind's pointing finger stabbed a pathway. "Dix climbs up that tree, then makes his way to the chimney ledge. There are plenty of handholds. It's quite easy, really."

"I'm sure."

Swinging himself up into the lowest branches, Stephen began his ascent. It was, as Rosalind had said, easy enough. And for an agile child like Dix, who practised the arboreal feats of a monkey, probably even easier. Most of the higher part of the wide stack had crumbled away at this section, and it proved but a short scramble from the tree to the top.

"There's a grating. Inside," called Rosalind. "To stop things falling down. Dix has built himself a kind of nest on it."

Stephen hauled himself to the top of the chimney, and caught a cold catspaw of breeze across his face and shoulders. His clothes were damp with sweat, but the involuntary shiver he gave was as much from apprehension as cold. He glanced over the side, down into the stack where the grid was fixed, almost afraid of what might be lying there.

And then he saw it.

A dark shape crumpled beneath him, its limbs thrown out at unnatural angles in an ungainly, sickening fashion. There was neither sound nor movement.

A wave of nausea swept him. The air was suddenly dark

before his eyes, the blood pounding in his ears. Round him, the sky dipped and dazzled in splintered bursts of light and darkness, and he was forced to take a deep, steadying breath before bending forward again to peer down at Dixon's eyrie.

The breath eased out on a sigh. A tree branch! That was all. It was the branch of a tree splayed on the platform below him. There were twigs and leaves, a piece of sacking – but no child. The chimney was empty.

Stephen began to function normally once more. Glancing down at his hands he saw that they were shaking. Slowly, he raised his head and scanned the sky, where wisps of cloud hung tranced in the stillness; he looked through the flickering green of the leaves beneath him, to the bright head by the foot of the tree, then out at the world beyond and below. The earth was dressed in its colour again. Dix was not dead in the chimney. Dix could be in any one of a dozen places – alive and well. Euphoria swept over him, and he swung himself down the side of the stack with almost reckless abandon.

Rosalind was staring up at him, the westering sun held in her hair, in a web of light.

"He's not there?"

"No," replied Stephen gently. "And perhaps that's just as well, because, after all the noise we've been making, it could only have meant that he was badly hurt."

"Do you think he is? Hurt?"

"No. Probably skylarking somewhere," Stephen reassured her, but for himself there was no such reassurance. Unless the child had returned home while they were searching, the affair would have to be put in professional hands.

He felt suddenly very tired.

In silence, they jogged their way back towards the village.

But even as Stephen and Rosalind came down from the hills, it was already too late. It had been too late from the very beginning. Because, by the time Rosalind started her search early that Sunday morning, Dixon Taggard had already been dead for more than twelve hours.

Four

It was the most shocking accident, everyone in the village agreed upon that – and the inquest was later to bear out that unanimous verdict. Death by Misadventure.

For, early that Sunday evening, a night and a day after his death, Dixon Taggard's body was discovered by some hikers at the foot of the terrifying outcrop of rock known as Lamia's Leap, two miles from Ardinford and in quite the opposite direction from where Stephen and Rosalind had been investigating the old smoke outlet.

The Leap was a quiet, unfrequented spot, visited only by climbers and naturalists, and had little to commend it, except that it was off the beaten track. There was no glorious view from its summit, no pretty picnicking area among its woods: it was known only for its high, cragged rock, its rare mosses, and the variety of its fungi. There was no reason in the world, as far as anyone could see, why Dixon should have decided to spend his Saturday evening there.

"He wouldn't," said Rosalind. Stephen looked at her face, closed, whey-coloured, and somehow incredibly haggard. But she would volunteer nothing further, and the only course open to him was to take her to her home. And, once there, what was there to say? I'll see you tomorrow, perhaps? But he watched her go in without a word.

Tongues wagged in the Red Lion that evening; wagged across fences, up and down lanes, into telephone receivers, and in and out of every dwelling within a radius of five miles or more.

Yes. The affair was indeed shocking, tragic, the most appalling waste of young life, but it was, nevertheless, an accident. The Taggards, mother and father, might be censured for their lack of care and control of their young, the village might blame itself for its own laxity in coming forward to search for the boy. But his death was still an accident. The proof was there, on and beside the Leap; the point where the child had climbed over the edge, the shreds of clothing on the cliff-face, displaced stones, scrapes and scratches, and the bush torn from the rock when he fell. The child's passage was there, sure enough, marked as clearly as if it had been traced in his own blood: he had tried to climb down the cliff, and he had fallen. It was as simple as that.

The only unanswered question was, why?

But, then, when did a young Taggard, or, indeed, any adventurous youngster, need a reason for risking life and limb? It was a childish prank that had had disastrous consequences, that was all.

There was one peculiar side-light: Dixon Taggard's pocket had been bulging with mint toffees. The boy himself had not purchased them, and everyone in Ardinford denied giving them to him. So? Odd. Had they, then, been stolen from somewhere?

"Not from me," said Mrs Drummond emphatically, later admitting, with reluctance, that she had sold similar mint toffees to Cynthia Chubb, at lunchtime, on the afternoon of the pageant. Miss Chubb was firmly sealed behind her own front door, and could hardly be faulted if Dixon Taggard had tumbled to his death with a pocketful of her sweets.

But why, then, thought Stephen, had Cynthia Chubb denied seeing the boy? That, however, was a question he was unable to answer, either then, or the following morning when he woke to a mist-locked sun and a head full of unresolved puzzles.

Besides, Miss Chubb would see no reason to satisfy his

curiosity. She said little, did not gossip, and had a disconcerting habit of tossing forth odd observances that appeared irrelevant to whatever was on hand. Rosalind's words came back to him, fluting through his brain, her disparaging opinion of Miss Chubb's mental powers, until, with the ghostly voice still ringing in his ears, he glanced up and saw Rosalind herself, a small wraith wrapped in the last rags of morning mist, standing in his garden.

She looked much the same as always – possibly a shade paler – untidy, uncombed, and with hands even more grimed than usual. Even from his window, Stephen could see earth clinging to her fingers, and realized that she must have been digging up plants of some kind, for she had a trowel and some roots in her hands.

"Mr Brand," she called, when she saw him staring out at her, "are we still going into Redeham, this morning?"

He flung open the window, uncertain how to treat her, or how far to offer sympathy. In the end, he took his cue from her and carried on in as natural a manner as he could.

"Do you still want to go to the swimming-baths?"

She nodded. "You said you wanted to time the lengths today."

"Yes, but –" He stared at her hands. "What have you got there?"

"Plants for dyeing. For my wool." He found they were back to the medieval project which his class had been pursuing for a couple of terms and which had culminated in the pageant. Sheep's wool, gathered from the fences and hedges, spun and woven by hand, and dyed from plants and herbs and roots, the whole process part of a way of life and a culture long gone, fascinating now, where once it had been survival. "Bramble roots for orange dye, and agrimony for yellow, isn't that right, Mr Brand?"

"Yes." He grinned. "As you probably know better than I do, Rosie Taggard, if you recall everything your Grannie taught you." He closed the window, and went outside to the waiting girl, thinking of Sarana Taggard, the matriarch, who still lived the life of the roving tinker, with all its close contacts with the countryside.

The sun was breaking through more hotly now, and the hedgerows were steaming.

"Are we going into Redeham by bus?" enquired Rosalind. "I can't see your car."

"It's not back from the garage yet. I shall have to phone from the village before we go into town, to check if it's ready." There were no such amenities as telephones in the two old farm cottages. "The rest of the swimming team is supposed to be meeting me on the Green at nine o'clock."

"They won't be there," said Rosalind enigmatically.

"What are you, then, some kind of sibyl?" He looked down at her. "And for goodness' sake put some of that soil back where it belongs before I take you on our public transport. Someone might imagine you belong to me."

Rosalind contemplated her dirt-engrained hands.

"Can I use your sink, Mr Brand? You 'ave 'ot water."

"All right, but be quick about it."

"Oh, thank you very much, Mr Brand." Rosalind flashed her blue-eyed smile.

"My deed for the day." He watched with amusement as she gushed hot water into the basin and began to wash her hands and face, building up lather into a creamy wave across her hair. She sang in tuneless accompaniment.

"Steady with that soap, girl," adjured Stephen. "You're not shampooing the next champion of Crufts, you know." Tossing her a towel, he stepped outside into the sunshine to wait until she had finished her ablutions.

He supposed he should have a word with her mother and father, and offer them his condolences, although he did not know how to shape the words and, in the event, it hardly mattered for the Taggards barely listened to his stumbling attempts at sympathy. Eventually, he placed a treasury note beside Mrs Taggards' hand, stuttering: "Please, buy something for the children," as if it were a birthday, or celebration of some kind, he thought miserably, and was immediately overcome with embarrassment. However, it was impossible to insult the Taggards. Mrs Taggard swept the note into her apron pocket with scarcely a glance.

"I hope," said Stephen, recovering, "that it is still all right to take Rosalind to the baths in Redeham? The teaching hour was already arranged, and she seems keen to go. It may serve to take her mind off" – he stumbled – "things."

Digger Taggard nodded and, dark-jowled and filthy-collared, followed him across the back garden – which always looked to Stephen as if some particularly ghastly war of attrition had recently been fought across its acreage – and stood by the dividing fence while the younger man climbed through.

"For ten quid," said Taggard, staring at Stephen with little bloodshot eyes, "you can teach the little bitch anything you like – teacher!" He coughed, and spat over the side of his boot. "Get me? For ten quid," he grinned, sticking his thumbs in his belt, and his voice took on an insinuating tone, "I can turn a blind eye to all your little goings-on – teacher! ... That's what they call it, ain't it, when it's done by the likes of you? Teaching? Nature-bloody-study? Out in the woods with all the little girls? But my kind, my Joseph, they put in jail." He gave a harsh laugh and rubbed his hand raspingly across his jaw.

Speechless, white-faced, Stephen stared at Taggard as if he would like to choke him.

Taggard leered. "We all know it's the little girls you're fond of – teacher! – for all you've that fine rectory skirt in tow. But there's a law against that sort of thing, isn't there? With little girls? But with our Rosie, now –"

"Pa!" Richlyn Taggard had come up behind his father. "Pa –" he protested again.

The older, heavier man swung back his fist and caught the lad a blow on the cheekbone that sent him reeling.

Stephen could stand no more. He felt physically sick.

Fortunately, Digger Taggard had finished, too; he had

remembered the money in his wife's pocket, and now he lurched on his heel and shambled back to his cottage to reclaim it.

Richlyn picked himself up without a word, and disappeared into the dilapidated shed behind him.

Holding tightly to his temper, Stephen walked slowly to his front gate and leaned there, head down, swallowing bile and trying to bolster his self-control. When he eventually glanced up it was to see Cynthia Chubb staring at him, wide-eyed, from the opposite side of the road. Her bicycle was propped against the hedge. God! thought Stephen. She must have seen and heard everything.

And what did she want?

Two or three times she ran the tip of her tongue across her lips and made a small step towards him, but each time she faltered back into the hedge.

In the end, Stephen said, in as kind a tone as he could muster at that moment: "Can I help you, Miss Chubb?"

"Yes, I —" She came towards him, plucking with her left hand at the pocket of her coat. "Mr Brand ..." Her eyes rolled slightly. "Would you —? ... You see —" She paced a step nearer, still plucking nervously at her pocket, then blurted out: "The cat —" She got no further for, looking over Stephen's shoulder, her eyes seemed to dilate and she stopped in mid-sentence and mid-step. Then she bolted back towards her bicycle. Without another glance in his direction, she grabbed her handle-bars, scrambled on to her saddle, and began to pedal away from him as fast as her legs would move, her coat billowing behind her like a sail.

Stephen was suddenly aware of Alison's familiar light perfume, and turned to find Rosalind standing at his elbow.

He smiled. "I see you found Miss Hunter's scent spray."

"Oh." Her face dropped. "I thought it was yours, it was on your window-sill."

His lips twitched. "Rosie, my love, I don't normally go around scented like a sweet-pea."

She gave a little giggle and flicked her lashes at him. "I

do now, though … What were you talking about to Crazy-Daisy?" She nodded in the direction of Miss Chubb's fast-disappearing back.

"Miss Chubb, to you."

"Miss Chubb, then … What cat?"

"I have no idea, you interrupted our not-very-illuminating conversation. I don't even know if she finished the word. She could have meant cat, short and simple – as in, here, kitty, kitty – or cat as in cat-o'-nine-tails, or catamaran, or catastrophe –"

"Or catalogue, or catapult, or cat-burglar," went on Rosalind, warming to the theme. "Anyway," she shrugged, "I don't suppose it's important, she's always coming out with silly remarks like that. The only thing she's any good at is singing hymns in church, and Mr Flowerdew says she sings like an angel." She sniffed. "She'll break her angelic neck some day batting around on that old bike."

Rosalind." Stephen's remonstrance was half-hearted, and he was staring along the now-empty road with his brows pulled together in a frown. "Something else –" He switched his gaze to Rosalind. "Of course – Angel … The destroying angel!"

"They're poisonous," said Rosalind.

Stephen stared at her.

"The Destroying Angel," said Rosalind. "It's the name of a toadstool."

"Oh. Miss Chubb mentioned it recently."

"They have chalky-white caps and are very poisonous. My Grannie says we're not to touch them."

"Then Miss Chubb wouldn't gather them to eat?"

"Not unless she was in a hurry for wings and a harp," grinned Rosalind. "Anyhow, there'd be none around at this time of year, they're an autumn toadstool. They grow up on the Leap –" Her voice faltered.

But another bell was ringing in Stephen's brain. He said: "What would there be around now to eat? In the way of toadstools, I mean? Miss Chubb did have some, she showed me a basketful last week, a summer fungus, and she'd gathered it from somewhere near the Leap."

"We don't like toadstools," said Rosalind. "Grannie Taggard still collects them and eats them because she's set in the old ways, but we prefer egg and chips." She considered. "There would be Deceivers about, I think, and Grey Caps."

"Grey Caps?"

She nodded. "Thin stalks, flattish caps. Grey. I don't like them much, but Grannie boils them up and –"

"Grey Caps –" He thought for a moment. "They sound about right. Would they also be called Grisettes?"

Rosalind shrugged.

"Yes," mused Stephen, "that's it. That's what Miss Chubb had in her basket. I remember now. She called them Grisettes. And she said there were plenty more where they came from."

"Up on the Leap?"

"Would they grow there?"

"I expect so," said Rosalind. "All kinds of queer things grow up there, my Grannie says ... Mr Brand –" She turned and grasped Stephen's arm, and laid her cheek against his sleeve. "Dix wouldn't have gone up there on his own, Mr Brand, really he wouldn't. Everyone says he was larking about, trying to climb the cliff, Mr Brand. But he wouldn't! He wouldn't!"

Stephen put his arm round her shoulders.

"Perhaps Dix had gone to gather toadstools for Miss Chubb, have you thought of that? Maybe that's why he was up on the Leap."

"Dix would never have been picking any old toadstools for Miss Chubb."

"He might," said Stephen slowly, "if she'd promised him some sweets as a reward."

"Not up there, he wouldn't," insisted Rosalind. "You ask Miss Chubb. She'll say she never asked Dix to do anything like that – and never gave him any sweets, either."

And, of course, Rosalind was right, reflected Stephen. Miss Chubb would deny it all, because Miss Chubb was frightened out of her wits. And why? Because she had bribed the child with sweets, and he had fallen? It appeared the only plausible explanation.

But, then, Dixon Taggard had not fallen from the cliff top, had he? Not from the top. He had been trying to climb down, hadn't he? And why should he have attempted to do that?

"He wouldn't have gone there," said Rosalind, on a rising note. "He'd never have gone there, Mr Brand. The place is cursed."

Stephen flicked a glance at the child. She seemed very close to tears. "All right," he said gently.

But Rosalind was past control. "He'd never have gone up there, I tell you. Never! Never! He was scared of that place. Scared to death –"

Stephen tried to picture Dixon Taggard afraid, and failed utterly. Dixon Taggard who would have walked through the graveyard at midnight without turning a hair – and frequently had.

Rosalind said, wailing: "It was the curse, you see. We all kept away from that place, because of the witch's curse."

Stephen looked puzzled. But he was conscious that the Taggards were of tinker stock, with heaven only knew what strange beliefs rooted in them.

"Cursed be ye that curse me, and cursed be ye that testify against me, and cursed be ye that persecute me ..." intoned Rosalind in a singsong voice.

It was then that Stephen recalled one of the old tales – some demented female or other who had been denounced as a witch, and sentenced to be hanged. And where, in these ancient villages, was there not some such memory or folktale handed down? Only, the Ardinford woman had not been hanged. She had screamed her curses and leaped from the highest rock. The Lamia's Leap. Of course! Stephen suddenly understood. Lamia. The old name for sorceress, enchantress, witch.

He pictured the place, the high, rocky plateau with its backing of dense woodland – that peculiar type of brooding, dark, wet woodland which contrives to smell sour no matter what the season or however hot the sun – the kind of terrain self-suited to attract the eerie reputation it undoubtedly had. The usual stories of suicides and driven death, of curses and vile deeds too nebulous to name. An atmosphere of menacing evil that stretched back into the mists of time.

"And cursed be bird and beast and byre ..." The words came oddly from Rosalind's lips, but she had learned her lesson well, learned at the knee of old Sarana who, in turn, had probably learned from her own grandmother.

"And cursed be crop and kin and fire ..."

"Yes, all right. Thank you, Rosalind," said Stephen. But Rosalind was now in full spate.

"And cursed be field and –"

"Yes. Thank you. Rosalind! The point is made. Dix would never have gone to Lamia's Leap."

"No," agreed Rosalind, glassy-eyed.

So – what had happened? In spite of Rosalind's protests to the contrary, Dix *had* gone to the accursed place. But under duress? Or fleeing from something more terrible, even, than the witch's malediction?

"Perhaps she chased him there," said Rosalind viciously.

"Miss Chubb? Oh, Rosalind, you can't be serious! You've got to have a reason for chasing a little boy – you don't just do it for fun."

"Perhaps she had a reason."

"Rosalind, Miss Chubb wouldn't have chased him anywhere, she had only to offer him a bag of sweets and he'd have gone with her into her own house like a lamb. Besides, I think he liked her –"

"Well, those men, then. Perhaps they chased after him, and caught him, and –"

"Men? What men?"

Rosalind burst into tears.

"Oh, oh, oh ..."

Stephen said grimly: "Yes, 'oh, oh, oh', indeed. What men, Rosalind?"

"The men who chased him that other time, when he pinched the case."

"What case?" God, he was beginning to sound like a damned parrot.

"The case in the car."

"What car? ... Oh, hell! Rosalind! Tell me the tale from the beginning."

Sniffling and snuffling, Rosalind began.

"It was Saturday morning, see –"

"No, I don't see," said Stephen icily, "but no doubt I might find enlightenment – eventually. Go on."

"Do you want to see the case?" She looked up at him woefully, blue eyes drenched.

"Yes. That might be an idea," said Stephen, his voice tight.

Rosalind trailed over to the Taggard shed, and trailed back again carrying a slim, black leather briefcase. The lock-strap had been cut.

"Is this the case?"

She nodded.

"All right. Carry on."

"Well, early Saturday morning, the morning of the pageant, that was, Dix was near Captain Sugden's west drive. You know it's hardly ever used, and the brambles and bracken are thick on either side of it. Dix had a long warren inside the ditch there, where he used to hide and play." She pushed back the long hair from her face. "Well, Saturday morning, he saw this car, see. A big black one. It pulled up in the drive, and Dix said there were four men inside. One of them, the boss it was, told the others to wait where they were till he came back, and he went off in the direction of the house, Sugden Court, I mean. The other men then got out of the car and began to stroll up and down the drive, and one picked some wild strawberries, Dix said, and –"

"Go on," said Stephen sternly.

"You won't be cross with me, Mr Brand?" wept Rosalind.

"Very probably." He looked at her in despair. "Why on earth didn't you tell me all this sooner?"

She wept louder. "I didn't think it mattered."

"You knew it did."

Rosalind flinched. "When the men were quite a way from the car, Dix pulled himself up on to the driveway, on the side where he couldn't be seen, and looked inside the car – all the doors were wide open, Mr Brand. They shouldn't have left the doors wide open, should they, Mr Brand?"

"Go on," said Stephen remorselessly.

"Well, that's all, really. Dix reached in, by the driver's seat, and took that case and ran off with it, and ducked into his hidden ditch, and away. I think the men must have heard him moving, or they might have caught a glimpse of him, or something, because Dix said they shouted and tried to chase him, but he gave them the slip easily. Dix said they sounded very mad."

"Quite likely."

"Dix said they were there on Saturday afternoon, at the pageant. He told me he saw them, but I don't know what happened after that because when it was all over I couldn't find my brother." She turned and held tightly to Stephen. "They wouldn't have gone after my brother for that, would they, Mr Brand? Not for an old case?"

"What was inside?"

"Nothing."

"Nothing? Nothing at all? No documents, no papers, or anything?"

"No. At least, Dix said it was just rubbish."

"Rubbish!" What could there be, conceivably, that a

Taggard would regard as rubbish? "Just papers, he meant?"

"I don't think so. He'd have kept paper – to draw on. He just said rubbish, and that he'd thrown it away because he didn't want any more."

"Any more what?"

"Rubbish, I suppose."

"And you have no idea what it could have been?"

"No. I've told you. He didn't want it, so he threw it away."

"Have you any idea where he threw it?"

"No." Her arm moved slightly "Well, somewhere in the churchyard, I think." There was a pause. Then: "There was a duster in the case. Dix said I could have it." She bent her head and scrabbled in her shoulder-bag, eventually pulling out a piece of chamois leather.

Stephen took it from her and looked at it thoughtfully. He slipped it into his pocket and straightened up.

"All right, Rosie, my love, we'd better return this to its rightful owner."

"If you're thinking about telling Sergeant Leach, he's away. He went off early this morning to a multiple pile-up this side of Redeham, Richlyn says."

"Damn!" Stephen hefted the briefcase in one hand. "I suppose Captain Sugden would be our best bet, then. The men in the car might have been visitors of his. Perhaps we can sort this out quietly."

However, as they entered the village, Sugden passed them in his Land-Rover, racing off in the direction of Redeham. He put up a hand to them as he flashed by, but was gone before they could attract his attention any further.

"Mrs Drummond knows and sees everyone," said Stephen. "We'll ask if she's heard anything about a missing briefcase."

Together, they galloped along the street.

As they passed George Flowerdew's cottage they noticed that the old man was once more painting his front door.

The canary-yellow had almost gone, covered by a coat of deep, soft green – an improvement to the eye, if a capitulation of the spirit.

In the tiny post office-cum-general stores, they found Mrs Drummond filling several large cardboard boxes with groceries and chocolate bars for the construction-gang who were at work at Sugden Court. The pick-up truck was outside, waiting to be loaded with this merchandise, and its driver was in the telephone box.

Mrs Drummond had heard nothing about any missing bag, and was of the opinion that an empty briefcase could be of little importance, but she offered to display the case in a prominent position in her shop.

"After all," she said reasonably, "everyone in this area comes in here, sooner or later."

Five

"Are we still going into Redeham?" queried Rosalind.

"Yes. On the next bus. I must see Alison and check what time she wishes me to pick her up tomorrow, and" – Stephen glanced at the occupied telephone box – "she'll let me use the rectory phone to ring Butt's garage." He pushed the reluctant Rosalind forward. "You can come along with me. And smile."

"I've told you, she don't like me."

"I think you're the one who is doing the disliking. Couldn't you join one of her clubs, or something?"

"Hell, no. You mean her old Brownies, or Guides, or her soppy old Sunday School?"

"You're a heathen, Rosie Taggard. You could be a great help to Miss Hunter."

"I help you, don't I?" said Rosalind, with disarming truth.

"You do, indeed." He smiled slightly. "Can you solve the mystery of our missing swimming team?"

Rosalind glanced around the Green.

"Well, for one thing, you're *late*," she said accusingly. "And for another, they've probably gone to Captain Sugden's place. They're not going to pay the bus fare to go swimming when they can get in free, are they?"

"I wanted to time the events," said Stephen. "Sugden's pool is a different shape and size."

Rosalind grinned. "Then you'll have to make do with me."

They swung off across the Green towards the rectory, shawled in its rambling roses and clematis and cascades of wistaria. The drowsy hum of bees came from every side.

Mary Witherspoon opened the door to them and ushered them into the large sunny room overlooking the rear garden of the rectory where she had been drinking coffee with Alison and the rector.

"Coffee, Stephen?" enquired Alison, coming forward with a smile. Her lips brushed his. Her skin was smooth and cool as water.

"Yes, thank you." He thought how attractive she looked, how restful. Dependable. There was about her an air of sturdy self-reliance.

She was small and slender, with a well-shaped figure and a firm line to her jaw, and she held herself proudly as befitted one who was able to trace an ancestry back to the first Crusades. Her nose was straight; her eyes were wide-apart, very large and calm and clear, their colour changeable according to mood or the luminosity of the day: ash-blue, ash-grey, like woodsmoke or the colour of a mist at sea. She was wearing a grey skirt and a crisp, long-sleeved white blouse, and her hair, which was fair and glittering like silver-gilt where the sun touched it, fell behind her shoulders, caught back by a black ribbon instead of folded into its customary neat pleat.

She looked young, cool, and very pretty, and about as accessible as the moon.

Alison turned to the child. "Coffee, Rosalind?"

"No ... Thank you. Can I use your bathroom?"

"Yes, of course." Alison indicated the door with her hand. "Straight up the stairs, and the first door on your right. Come, I'll show you the way." Gracefully, she moved across to the child, and Stephen watched them leave the room together. Fire and ice. The two extremes in colouring, temperament, and upbringing, as different as it was possible for two people to be. It was small wonder that there was no love lost between them.

Kelvin Hunter's eyes, too, were on his daughter; those strange, light eyes which seemed to look right through a man and find him wanting. Stephen often wondered why the rector had been content to remain in such a backwater as Ardinford. And he remembered Mary Witherspoon's caustic comment when he had once aired his puzzlement. "It suits Kelvin," Mary had said. "Big frog in a little puddle." With a start, Stephen returned to the present and understood that Hunter was addressing him.

"– Dreadful business."

"Yes," Stephen agreed, hazily. "Dreadful."

"You know, of course, that everyone in the village is castigating Miss Chubb? Ridiculous, isn't it? But events in her past are against her, and then there were those sweets, and they must have someone to blame, I suppose. Although we all know that Dixon Taggard suffered with wanderlust."

"Yes," agreed Stephen again, unable to think of anything more scintillating to say.

"Perhaps you could arrange to have a word with the children in your class, when you see them again, and insist that they stop their cruel baiting of the poor woman."

Stephen had a devilish impulse to answer: "Aye, aye, sir!" But in the interests of good relationships he thought it healthy to restrain it. Instead, he said: "Yes ... I will." The conversation dried. He was never at ease with his future father-in-law. After a few moments, he tried again. "I see George Flowerdew has changed the colour of his door once more. Green. Very pleasant."

"Oh ... Yes." The rector's eyes gleamed like a cat's.

Mary Witherspoon's cup clicked down on its saucer.

"And how," she said, "did you arrange that?"

The rector said, with a faint smile playing across his lips: "A little persuasion, Mary."

"Persuasion! Is that what you call it?"

"My dear, I hardly twisted his arm. I promised him one of my Louise Hunter roses, that's all. He's coveted one for years and the plants are not available on the general market."

"So?"

"Well, I couldn't allow my glorious hunting-pink Louise to be put near a canary-yellow door. You must admit yourself that the effect would be disastrous – garish in the extreme."

"Bosh! And June is not the month for lifting roses."

"No. But I've earmarked one for him in November – to give him the chance to change his paint."

"Blackmail!"

"Mary! What a nasty word ... Say, diplomacy, rather. And effective, I think."

"Yes, very," said Mary Witherspoon, "as George Flowerdew's roses are his life's hobby."

But Stephen could not help wondering what would have happened if the rebel had continued to preach rebellion.

Hunter said: "Flowerdew is very like my grandfather, a difficult old man – obstinate, under a cloak of easy-going insouciance; not given to careful thought; rather slow, at times –" He poured himself another cup of coffee and stirred it, thoughtfully. "You remind me of my grandfather, Stephen."

"On his better days, I trust," said Stephen, stifling a smile.

Hunter's eyes flicked upwards, and Mary Witherspoon cut in with: "Stephen, I hear your archery butts broke all financial records. the whole village was delighted with them. Great fun."

Hunter said smoothly: "Yes, most enjoyable. Fortunately, we're very easy to please."

"I wanted to try something that hadn't been done in Ardinford before," explained Stephen. "Only, it's difficult to come up with anything really original, isn't it?"

"Not if one's of normal intelligence, I should have thought," said the rector.

Stephen, drinking his coffee with quite commendable

restraint, caught the brown eyes of Mary Witherspoon over his cup and gave her a rueful wink. Hunter was the kind of man who excelled at everything, including putting down young men who had the temerity to court his daughter. Stephen studied his future father-in-law. Tall, handsome, with clear-cut features and strongly-marked dark brows, and a mane of thick, silver hair. The eyes were an uncomfortably clear, light arctic-blue. It was a strong face, an uncompromising face; arrogant, even – the face of someone who knew what he wanted and usually got it. The face of someone whom it would be wise to keep on one's side.

A shadow fell across the table, and Stephen turned his head and saw that Alison had come back into the room, silently, and alone.

"Where's Rosalind?" he asked. "Not still in the bathroom?"

Alison's lips quirked. "She's having a wash."

"Another one!" said Stephen, incredulously.

"I think perhaps our toilet facilities have more to offer than your kitchen sink," said Alison, her smile growing broader. "There's a very feminine little girl under that rough exterior."

"Well, I hope to goodness she hurries up, we've already missed one bus." He added, on a sigh: "I'm sorry she's always so rude to you."

Alison lifted her shoulders in a slight, graceful movement. "She's jealous, that's all."

"I don't see why."

"Don't you?" murmured Alison in an enigmatic tone, gathering the empty cups on to a tray.

As Stephen moved to help her, he suddenly caught sight of the rector. Kelvin Hunter was standing quite still, his hands clenched whitely at his sides, watching Alison – and he was staring at his daughter with undisguised hunger in his eyes.

Possibly he felt Stephen's puzzled gaze upon him because

he stepped forward at once, and said: "Alison, my dear, while I remember – I saw Ellery Sugden this morning and he asked me to tell you that the upper meadow and the chalk quarry will have to be out-of-bounds to everyone. That goes for your Brownies, too, I'm afraid ... He has men excavating roads and things, and there are diggers and dumpers and earth-scoops milling around, and he doesn't want any of the children having an accident. I think the construction-gang is using the quarry as a base, for their huts and equipment."

"Then he might have told us earlier. We are supposed to be holding a two-day camp there, next weekend – similar to the one we had last year." Alison looked annoyed. "It's all arranged. My Brownies are too young to go any further afield, and anywhere closer would land them in their own back yards." She flashed her father a half-hearted smile. "I shall have to cancel my visit to Veronica, and try to arrange something."

"That won't be necessary," said the rector quickly. "Ellery would like to see you this afternoon, at the Court. He has a suggestion to make."

"I'll bet he has," said Mary Witherspoon.

Hunter ignored her. "I think he's going to offer you his cherry orchard as a camping ground, well away from the construction work."

"That should take care of the food and recreation problems," said Mary Witherspoon. "Supply and demand unlimited, and plenty of cherry-stones for the little dears to spit in each other's eyes."

"I'll phone Ellery," said Alison. "There's no need to pay him a visit."

"He wants to see you," insisted Hunter.

Alison flung a quick glance at Stephen while looking as if she wished to argue.

Tactfully, Stephen said: "I've just remembered – may I use your telephone, please, Alison?" And he went past her into the hall to place a call to Butt's garage. On his left, open, was the oak door of Hunter's study, with the silver cups for this and that, and the burnished shield above the desk: "VICTOR LUDORUM".

Stephen smiled grimly. Very apt. Victor over all. Or, to put it more bluntly – Top Dog. He lifted the receiver.

Meanwhile, in the room behind him, Alison returned to the business in hand.

"It's not convenient for me to visit Sugden Court today. Why has Ellery this sudden desire for my company?"

Hunter smiled. "He was always very set on you, Alison."

"Or possibly on my share of my grandmother's money," returned Alison.

"Well," said Mary Witherspoon, "he seems to have plenty of money of his own, now. From being almost penniless, and having to sell land to pay his debts and the upkeep of Sugden Court, he's now ordering renovations and new buildings, and is planning to open the place to the public. That must be costing a fortune."

"I imagine he's hoping to recoup," said Alison. "He's expecting the venture to be a great success."

Mary Witherspoon gave a short laugh. "Is he indeed? Then I hope he has something better in mind than those moth-eaten flamingoes on his lawn."

"Still," said Alison. "it is very kind of him to allow the children to use his pool for the summer."

"I dare say," said Mary Witherspoon, with a glance at Hunter, "that he's hoping it will keep them out of more inconvenient mischief elsewhere."

Hunter frowned. "Sugden's an excellent fellow."

"You didn't always think so," said Alison, in a quiet voice.

"You were very young, then," replied the rector.

"And Stephen wasn't firmly entrenched in our back garden," put in Mary Witherspoon. She turned challengingly to Kelvin Hunter, a deadly glint in her eye.

"And your sudden partiality for Sugden wouldn't have anything to do with the fact that his accident pretty well castrated him, would it?"

There was a stunned silence.

After a few seconds, the rector said: "You have a waspish tongue, Mary. And it's time you learned to disregard general gossip." He swung on his heel and left the room, snarling as he slammed into his study: "Some of us have to do some work!"

"Whew," said Stephen, hovering in the doorway of the big sunny room. "Did I detect a faint note of criticism there? Who's upset the Reverend?"

"Mary," said Alison shortly.

"Oh," said Stephen. "I thought perhaps it was me ..." He came further into the room. "Butt says he's already delivered my car and left it outside my cottage, with the bill under the windscreen wiper, so I might as well go home and collect it, and proceed into Redeham under my own steam ... Alison, be a love and rustle up Rosalind for me. I think she must have fallen down the plughole."

"Yes, of course." Alison went quickly through the doorway.

Almost automatically, Mary Witherspoon caught Stephen's arm as he made to follow his fiancée. He glanced down at the plump, beautifully-shaped hand, and then at her face, in surprise.

"Take her away, Stephen," she said urgently. "Alison. Take her away as soon as you possibly can. Marry her, and get her away from here. Forget any ideas about living in the rectory afterwards, it just would not work."

"No," said Stephen ruefully. "I'm beginning to realize that, myself: my future father-in-law likes me not at all. Funny, though –" He paused, considering. "I thought he did, in the beginning. Though God knows what I've done to offend him."

"In the beginning," said Mary Witherspoon dryly, "you posed no threat. Kelvin thought you were out of Alison's league and that she'd never look twice at you."

Stephen grinned. "Then he was no more surprised than I was. Anyhow, perhaps he'll change his mind and learn to appreciate my lovely nature ... He's done an about-face with cousin Veronica, and with Sugden, so perhaps I'll be next on the good boys' list."

"No," said Mary sharply, and Stephen again looked at her in surprise. "He'll do everything he can to come between you both. Don't you see, Veronica and Sugden are lesser evils ... Stephen, I love the Hunters; Louise, his wife, was my best friend. But Kelvin is replacing her with Alison – in every way...."

Stephen stared at her without comprehension, then glanced up at the portrait above the fireplace. Louise. Yet it was Alison's face which smiled down at him, although softer, somehow, with more humour about the eyes and more warmth and compassion on the lips.

"He adored her," said Mary simply. "They adored each other. From the moment they met there was never anyone else for either of them, ever. When Louise died, I was so afraid –" She pulled herself together quite visibly, with a little shake. "A weaker man would, perhaps, have gone to pieces. But not Kelvin ..."

No, thought Stephen, not Kelvin Hunter, who could meet catastrophe head on and stand among the shattered fragments of his world and manipulate the splinters –

"But he changed," went on Mary. "Although I sometimes feel that we never really know anyone in depth at all. And now ... In his mind," she said patiently, "Alison is becoming Louise. His wife. I have watched it happening. And he has been without her for so long ..." She shivered. "Do you notice the way he looks at her? Do you understand what I am trying to tell you?"

Stephen's eyes darkened in shock. "That's a terrible thing to say."

"Nevertheless, it is the truth."

"He hardly touches her."

"He doesn't touch her, because he dare not touch her. And, so far, he knows it ... But when he breaks –"

"I can't believe it." Stephen moved restlessly. "And certainly Alison can have no idea –"

"The Sleeping Princess? Alison loves him," she said simply. "He's all she's ever had to love. But there is love and love. And I don't know what to do." There was a shake in her voice. "In you, I think she has glimpsed something she needs, however diffident she may appear to be. Stephen, she needs love, physical love, expressions of affection –"

Stephen looked at her helplessly. "Are you asking me to seduce Alison?"

"I don't know! I don't know!" she cried in anguish. "But it might not be such a bad idea, at that."

"Mary –"

"This visit to Veronica would be the perfect opportunity for you to spend some time alone together; Veronica would understand, she realized the danger, long ago, and tackled Kelvin. But she lost." Mary tightened her grip on his arm. "If you could at least persuade Alison to go with you, to spend some time with you, away from Ardinford, away from the rectory, away from her father ... I'll talk with her; I'll phone Veronica, and Veronica will throw her weight down on our side."

Stephen patted her hand, it was all he could do, for he could hear voices on the stairs. He was not as sure as Mary that he could persuade Alison to do anything at all; he was not even certain that he wanted to try.

"I'm ready, Mr Brand," said Rosalind's voice. "Miss Hunter says your car is back."

Rosalind's face was the colour of a freshly-boiled shrimp, and the ends of her hair were damp. She wafted towards him on a cloud of scented soap and talcum powder.

"I hope you've left things tidy," Stephen said, frowning at her before moving aside to speak to Alison.

"Oh, yes," Rosalind said happily. She skipped to the

door and turned to look over her shoulder. "Oh, do come on, Mr Brand. Hurry up."

With a grimace at his fiancée, and a thumbs-up sign to Mary, he followed the child out into the sunshine.

"Their bathroom's lovely," said Rosalind. "Everything is blue, and when you put water in the sink it reminds you of the swimming pool, and they have a towel there as big as a blanket." She swung her shoulder-bag round her head.

"I'm glad you enjoyed your trip, cheaper than the regular seaside, I suppose. But I wish you'd forgo this reprehensible desire to inspect other people's plumbing."

"You're not cross, are you, Mr Brand?" Rosalind's eyes sparkled. Her bag completed another circle.

"No, I'm not cross –" Unaccountably, his mood had risen to match hers, and he found himself striding along blithely beside her. "We'll cut through the churchyard," he said, his hand on the lychgate. Through the churchyard, and out into the meadows beyond. Lark free.

Ardinford church was small and flint-walled, with a squat tower; the churchyard, the newest portion, anyway, was neat and closely-clipped – if Dixon Taggard had, indeed, deposited his rubbish there it would soon be removed, probably had already been removed – only over the more ancient tombs in the disused part of the grounds was the grass waving its ripened seeds. Here and there, were the dark bulks of yews, centuries old, with thick, gnarled trunks and branches overspreading earth covered in dead needles. Horse-chestnut trees surrounded both graveyard and rectory, and the sun spangled down through the moving leaves, weaving patterns on the path and turning Rosalind's hair to flame.

She gave her arm another twirl, one so energetic that the bag shot from her fingers and described a high arc before landing upside-down on the grass. Several things spilled out. A container of talcum powder rolled to Stephen's feet. Lily-of-the-valley. He bent down and picked it up and handed it to Rosalind without a word.

Quickly, silently, she stuffed it back into the bag, picked up the rest of her things and hitched the bag over her shoulder. They walked on in silence. They reached the gate on the far side of the churchyard, went through. In silence still, they crossed the meadow, bright with early summer flowers, and climbed a five-barred gate. Here, dumbly and inexplicably, Rosalind turned to Stephen and, flinging herself at him, clutching, burst into tears. She sobbed as if she had suddenly found the world too much to bear.

"Hey, steady on," he said, his voice quiet. He pulled her gently against his chest and cradled her there, the childish curve of her cheek against his heart. Tenderly, he stroked her hair. "Hush," he said. "Hush. It's all right, Rosie."

Coughing, Rosalind scratched around in her bag, found the container of talcum powder and held it out to him.

"There," she hiccoughed, "give it back to her. It's hers ... But you knew it was, didn't you? I was going to keep it. She has so much stuff up there, I didn't think she'd miss it, but she might. And then she might blame you ... for taking me there." She wiped an arm across her eyes. "I'm sorry, Mr Brand. Will you put it back for me? You can say I picked it up by mistake." She gave another hiccough, but she met his eyes squarely with her own of that wild, lambent blue, before her head sank against him once more.

He nodded, a lump in his chest. He wanted to give her the talcum powder, to give her a whole crate full of talcum powder, to shower her with gifts, with perfume, with everything she wanted – but he knew he could not. He knew he would never be able to give her anything at all. He looked down at her.

Rosalind, of the long, fiery hair and the merry eyes, and the body that was thin and taut and not yet beginning to bud. And it came to him, then, that he never would be there to see Rosalind come into bloom. That soon she would be as far removed from him as the clouds which raked the sky. The thought made him infinitely depressed. On life's present showing of the dice she would probably be pregnant before she was sixteen, crushed, and perpetuating the life-style of the Taggards ...

And there was nothing he could do about it. Nothing.

Oh, God,. not Rosalind, he groaned inwardly, with her bright, quicksilver youth and the passionate promise of that generous mouth. Not Rosalind. Let her go free. Let her, at. least, escape the fate awaiting her in that feckless household –

He found he was trembling, his heart slamming beneath her cheek.

He could feel the warmth of her skin through his thin shirt, and forced himself to put her from him, watching as she climbed the gate at his side. Quite starkly, then, he realized that he was fonder of Rosalind than he had any right to be, and felt his world darken with horror. Was he really contemplating the child in the way Digger Taggard had so revoltingly suggested? Was he really, at base, twisted, a deviant of some kind, the kind of man who molested little girls? Stephen felt sick in the pit of his stomach. No, he told himself, Taggard was wrong. This was not a sexual thing at all. He wanted to protect her, cherish her, love her ... But perhaps they all said that?

"Wait there," he said harshly. He wheeled away blindly, and left her sitting on the top of the five-barred gate.

Rosalind watched his figure dwindle across the meadow to disappear under the shadow of the trees. She mopped her eyes. Lost in desolation, she did not hear the footsteps approaching until they were almost upon her. Three men, strangers, who stopped directly in front of the gate.

Warily, Rosalind eyed them, ready to run.

"It's all right, little girl," said the tallest. "We're not going to hurt you. We hope you might be able to help us."

Rosalind shook her head, poised to leap from her perch.

"Oh, I'm sure you can. You don't know what we want, yet," said the fattest of the men. "Just a little information, that's all –" He advanced towards her.

"Get on with it, Whooms," snarled the tall man, who

had eyes that were light and green and that frightened Rosalind. "This is the girl. She was in the post office a while ago with Ferris's briefcase. She's the boy's sister. She must know what he did with the stuff." He leaned forward, resting his hand on his knee. "You do, don't you?" he said. "Where is it? The bundle that was in the case your brother stole from us?"

"I don't know," said Rosalind. "I don't know what you're talking about."

"I think you do. And there's money in it for you, if you tell us." He brought out a five-pound note and swayed it in front of Rosalind's eyes. Hypnotized, she waited.

"Well?" he said at last.

"I don't know anything," said Rosalind obstinately.

"Do you know what happens to little girls who tell lies?" asked the man called Whooms.

Rosalind scowled back at him.

"Oh, come on," said his tall companion. "We haven't time for all this, we'll have to take a risk and nab her, and make her talk. There's no choice." He made a lunge at Rosalind and grabbed her shoulder.

It was a mistake. She twisted out of his grasp and dropped on the far side of the gate. Scrambling to her feet, she took to her heels and ran. Up the slope behind her, up the short, rabbit-bitten turf, with its stemless thistles, its rose-purple thyme, self-heal, and trailing yellow tormentil, up she went, running as if all the hounds of hell were at her heels.

There was a curse and, as one man, the three vaulted the gate and were after her, she could hear their feet thumping the ground behind her. The bank steepened, but Rosalind ran on, upwards, then, too late, realized her mistake. They were driving her away from the village, away from Stephen; they were chasing her, as they must have done Dix, cutting her off from help.

She swung out in a wide arc and began to curve downwards to her left, weaving among the stunted dogwood that offered no shelter. And again they headed her off. There was only one direction left open to her – downhill, through Tillett's Wood, a wild, unspoiled tract of oaks and beech and birch, interspersed with tangles of hawthorn and dark-leaved holly, that marched alongside the river.

The wood was cool, shaded; the sun dappling down through the trees. From within the shadowy recesses a ringdove purred. Following the path beside the river, Rosalind knew she was going further and further from the village, and twice attempted to cut up into the trees, but was headed off, back towards the purling water. Twice, too, she attempted to hide among the undergrowth, heedless of the tearing thorns, but panicked at the last moment, when her pursuers appeared to be coming straight towards her, and left her shelter to fly onwards again. Now there was only the chuckle of the shallow water over the stones, and the ringdove moaning. Everything else had fallen quiet; the rustles, the stirs, the cheeps and trills and calls, all quiet, as if insects and animals were holding their breath, watching this deadly game of hide-and-seek.

Rosalind scuttled on, her breath coming in terrified gasps, her heart thumping enough to burst her chest. The branches of the alders whipped against her, stinging her cheeks and hands. Once, she slipped, and her foot went into the stream. But the shock of the cold water brought her to her senses. To outwit the men she would have to use all her native cunning, her headlong flight was merely playing straight into their hands. They were strong, tough, determined, and there were three of them. In any direct contest it was obvious that they must win.

Rosalind scrambled up the slope once more, away from the river path, dodged round some heavy undergrowth, then twisted down towards the river yet again, under the alders where the big sympetrum dragon-flies darted and hovered over the water, red darning-needles in flight, and the alderflies shimmered thick as apple blossom. They rose

in clouds around her, then settled again. On she went,
beside the burdock and the butterbur with its huge,
rhubarb-like leaves that formed a canopy beneath which
nothing could grow. She halted. Gently, she parted the
stems and crawled forward, forward into the dim, deep
green cavern of filtered, rippling light; in, under the leaves,
softly, like some hunted creature of the woods. Then she
could go no further, the river was at her heels. Petrified, she
crouched, trying to still her panting breath, trying not to
shake with fear and make the tall leaves tremble. She sat
quite still, her hair full of fragments of burdock, hugging
her arms around herself, growing, she felt, smaller and
more insignificant by the minute. Even the ringdove had
ceased its purring, a sure sign that someone, something,
was coming, padding along on silent feet. Hunting.
Rosalind cracked her ears. The stillness was uncanny. She
could hear nothing. Nothing except the violent chattering of
her own teeth. Could see nothing through the curtain of
leaves.

Crouched in the green gloom of her hiding-place, the cool
scent of crushed water-mint rising from the river, Rosalind
tried to stifle the urge to run. Here it was safe, safe. She
closed her eyes.

The slow minutes halted by.

Somewhere, there was the snap of a twig, the rustle of
leaves. Her lashes flew wide. What? Where? Seconds
passed. Then the stems parted above her head, and eyes
like green glass stared down at her. And a hand shot out to
lock round her wrist, gripping it hard.

Six

Well over an hour was to pass before Stephen's feet turned in the direction of Tillett's Wood. Finding no sign of Rosalind near the gate where he had left her, he had continued on to his cottage, only to discover from one of her sisters that Rosalind had not returned there. He climbed into his car and drove back to the village and wasted further time there, searching for the girl, then, puzzled but not unduly worried, parked the car beside the Green and retraced his steps across the fields to the gate. He looked up and down. No sign, no clue. There was nothing anywhere to tell him in which direction Rosalind might have gone.

In the end, he vaulted the gate and took himself to the top of the slope. Again, nothing.

The hard straight sunlight lay across the thin turf, striking blinding whiteness from the patches of exposed chalk where the rabbit burrows honeycombed the ground. It was very hot; a pocket of shimmering, airless heat, like the arrid breath from an open oven.

Stephen stood, trying to put himself in the child's shoes. She had recently lost her brother; she had been distressed, unhappy; then, today, again upset and, perhaps, also a little ashamed. The smaller grief following upon the greater one had shaken her to the core ... So, what would she have done? Would she have wished to be alone?

Probably.

His eyes raked a wide semi-circle. The village before him, distant, huddled around its Green; the broad, shallow

stream running through the spreading meadows; a
sprinkling of cottages here and there, and clumps of trees,
and, away to his left, the cool, leafy tract of Tillett's Wood,
peaceful and all-enfolding.

He hesitated no longer.

Within the wood it was fresh and pleasant, the scent of
water-mint and marjoram adding a clean tang to the air.
He turned to follow the path beside the river.

On his left, the trees curved upwards, across earth half-
hidden in tangles of wild clematis and low-growing bushes.
To his right, beyond the green lushness of riverside plants
and trailing cords of honeysuckle, and alders, and the
feathery flowers of meadowsweet, slipped the shallow,
lovely Ardin, glittering in sunlight and flickering in shade.
The water was very clear, reflecting the trees in its smooth
current. He could see the pebbles on the bottom, and tiny
fish, dark transparencies, in shoals, freckling among the
water weeds, which were brilliant green and rose-copper,
and flowed in long tresses, like mermaids' hair.

Other than the soft thud of his feet loping over the
ground, there was no alien sound to disturb the peace. Just
the gentle chuckle of water as it lipped around its stones,
and the muted murmuring of insects and birds. Stephen
paced on.

The sunshine trembled in the leaves overhead, and
spilled downwards in showers of gold; a moving light that
dappled the path before him, quivering on a butterfly like a
blown leaf of summer blue; on a patch of yellow cress; on
another, brighter, whole tapestry of tiny flowers. He
stopped dead.

It was tapestry!

He was looking at a tapestry bag. Rosalind's shoulder-
bag.

Slowly, he stooped and picked it up. There was no
mistake: it was Rosalind's, all right. Deep inside himself,
Stephen felt an icy twist of fear. Rosalind never went
anywhere without that bag; it held the few – the very few –

treasures she possessed. It was quite unthinkable that she would have left it lying there. He bent again and gathered up the scattered, pathetic contents that had tumbled from the bag and put them back inside it. Something was missing but, for the moment, he could not think what it could be.

He looked around, half hoping to see the child come flying through the trees.

But there was no sign of anyone, or anything.

Because there seemed nothing else to do, he went on walking, peering from side to side, as if the plants and bushes and stones could give him some answers to this riddle. But there was no movement, no flash of racing colour among the trees, no delighted laughter. He called, and his voice bounded back to him heavily from trunk to trunk, an echoing sadness. He whistled, and no one came. He was just beginning to feel that he had passed that way before, that the day was turning into a recurring nightmare of another day, gone not so long ago, when he spotted the clump of broken butterbur. Someone had been along the path, and recently.

The tall plants had been smashed and flattened into a battlefield of dying leaves, and gave off a dark, weedy odour. The sliding glitter of water beckoned beyond.

Stephen thrust his way through the damaged plants until he came to the river's edge. The current moved serenely, reflecting the green and blue of tree and sky, and combing out the water weed.

As he edged to his left, along the lip of the riverbank, with the rampant plant-growth at his back, his foot slipped on some stems of scarlet pimpernel which had straggled down the slope, and he landed in the stream. Cursing mildly beneath his breath, he hauled himself out again and up on to the bank, emptied the water from his shoes, and then carried on his way.

Five minutes later, he was still walking, still calling, with nothing answering but the rippling stream. The river was

narrower here, boulder-strewn against its far bank, the
water curling whitely round the larger stones before flowing
free. The bank this side was steeper, too, treacherous with
plants and slippery grass, and a slim birch rose almost from
the water, blocking his passage. Stephen swung out and
round it, his eyes still on the precarious foot-hold under him.
He felt himself sliding again, and put out a hand to clutch a
plaited rope of honeysuckle. Looking down, he saw the
water just beneath him, a smooth, dazzling mirror at this
point, with the trailing fronds of the water weed waving
slowly from side to side in an idle, many-coloured motion.
There, emerald; here, red. Red as Rosalind's hair. It
streamed out in the current, a lovely copper-claret, like the
tresses of some nymph or naiad. There was a broken tendril
of honeysuckle beside it, floating lazily half in, half out, of
the water.

Stephen stood transfixed.

A couple of butterflies drifted upwards.

Below him, the mermaid's hair continued to wave
languorously to and fro, the ends coiling and uncoiling
like small beckoning fingers. And still he did not move.
Although his whole being was now crying out in anguish:
"Oh, no, oh, no! Rosalind, oh, no!"

He knew that she was dead. Even though he refused to
accept the fact, he knew that she was dead. She was lying
face downwards in the shallowest part of the stream, one
arm curved above her head, the other outflung at her side,
still grasping a snatch of honeysuckle-bine. And even death
could not drain the vibrant colour from her hair.

"Oh, dear God!" he groaned, and, released abruptly
from his trance, leaped down into the water. He bent and
gathered Rosalind into his arms, and she curved across
them, water showering from her hanging hair in sparkling,
sun-touched drops. She felt very light, her bones as fragile
as a bird's, and he lifted her to the bank with ease. He did
not know how long he worked over her, trying to restore
breath that had gone. He knew only that he had to try.

It was obvious where she must have fallen, for there was a scraped trail and debris down the bank, and he had seen the stone on which she had hit her head. The final irony, that. That it had taken but a few inches of water to drown her, Rosalind, who had been able to swim like a fish.

When all hope had died, he rose and, leaving her lying there, turned and ran.

He was beyond feeling. He had no recollection of retracing his path through the wood, nor of planning what he had to do next, but when, twenty minutes later, he shook off the daze which had clouded his senses, he was entering the rectory kitchen garden through the back gate.

His feet had carried him unerringly to Alison.

She was alone in the kitchen, sitting at the table, her head bathed in bright sunshine. When she saw Stephen she leaped to her feet. He looked like a ghost, harrowed and grey, and his chest was heaving painfully from the exertion of running every step of his way.

"What is it? What's the matter?" She pressed him down on to a chair before his legs could buckle beneath him.

"Alison ..." he said, fighting for breath. "Alison ..."

He told her then, everything, haltingly and between great gasping gulps for air. As he finished, Alison set a cup of scalding, sweet tea in front of him and told him to drink it. For a moment, he stared at the brown liquid as if he had forgotten where and who he was, then he lifted it to his lips. His hand was shaking, and his teeth chattered against the rim of the cup.

"And you are quite sure she is dead?"

"Yes." He could think of nothing else to say.

"From what you've told me, it appears certain that her death was an accident. But we must phone the doctor, now, and Sergeant Leach, to start with. I imagine he'll need to contact Redeham. Do you feel up to answering a few questions? They'll want you to do that, as you were the one who discovered the body." She spoke in her usual calm, unruffled manner. "And you'll probably have to take them there, to the spot where you found her ... Would you like me to inform Leach and Tom Blewitt?" Doctor Thomas Blewitt was a close friend of them both.

Stephen nodded, and she went quickly to the telephone, picked up the receiver, and began dialling.

When she came back to him, he had his head in his hands.

With all her heart, she wanted to comfort him, to banish that lost, blank expression which stared starkly from his eyes. But she had no idea of how to set about it, knowing only that he needed a softer nature than was hers to give.

Silently, she went across and sat beside him and, with an awkward, unaccustomed gesture because she had no gift for showing tenderness, put her arms around him and cradled his head against her breast. Blind, he turned his face to her, still shivering.

"It's shock," she said quietly. "That's all. You'll feel better in a minute. Tom will give you something, I expect."

"Oh, this is very cosy," said Kelvin Hunter, from the doorway. "I thought I heard voices."

Stephen glanced up, his eyes a grey cloud of incomprehension and grief.

In a few short sentences, Alison apprised her father of all that had happened.

"And you've sent for the doctor and Leach?"

"Yes, everything's been taken care of," Alison said, in her cool little voice. There were occasions when Stephen felt an urge to shatter that composure, roughly.

Hunter said: "That should have been attended to at once, before he came here." He stared at the younger man. "What else have you done?"

Momentarily, Stephen's eyes lost their blankness, and he gave a hard little laugh.

"All the wrong things, I'm afraid. I lifted her out of the water, and –"

"You moved her? That was a stupid thing to do," said

Hunter. "You should have touched nothing."

Stephen took a long moment to reply.

"I wondered if artificial respiration would help ..." His voice died. The words had sounded slurred and unsteady.

"It should have been obvious, from what you've told us," said Hunter, "that it was hopeless from the start."

"Maybe." Stephen turned and looked at Kelvin Hunter again, his face as grey as ashes. But the terrible dead expression had gone. His eyes were bitter and cold. The abrasive manner of the rector had at least served to pull him together as nothing else could have done. "I wasn't thinking as clearly as you might have done." He added no more, for there was the sound of a car outside, and then doors slamming.

After that, for Stephen it was a bewildering haze of questions and answers; a mad devil-dance of movement and faces and places, as he talked and walked, and pointed out the spot where he had found Rosalind in the river. And Rosalind herself. Although he could never remember, afterwards, ever really seeing her again.

He did recall, however, the ambulance standing in the road. And the sight of that gave him a violent kick to his stomach.

Doctor Blewitt accompanied him back to the rectory.

"Well," said Tom Blewitt, "it seems a pretty clear case of accidental death. The child slipped and hit her forehead on a rock and fell face downwards in the river. You can see what happened. She was still grasping a piece of broken creeper ... There will have to be a post mortem, of course, and an inquest, but they'll be mere formalities, I should think. There's no suspicion of foul play, and the child hardly committed suicide." He wheeled, his hand on the door. "There was just one thing, though. All the fingers on her right hand were broken. Odd." He gave a slight frown. "Presumably she must have done that when she fell. Anyhow, I imagine everything will soon be made plain to us, there's no need to worry. Come along, Stephen, I'll give you something to make you sleep tonight, you look terrible."

"I must collect my car from the Green," said Stephen. He turned and, like a man in a dream, walked from the room, swaying slightly as he went.

"I'll go with him," decided Hunter. "I wish to call on the Taggards to see if I can help them in any way. Those poor parents have now a double tragedy to cope with." And he followed Stephen and the doctor through the door.

Very much later, Mary Witherspoon arrived from the village with her own garbled version of the day's tragic events.

"The story is all over Ardinford," she said, "in some form or another."

"How can that be?" asked Alison.

"The ambulance was seen, of course, and the doctor and the police; that was enough to start tongues wagging. And then the more ghoulish amongst us made it their business to find out the rest by the usual process of rubbernecking," said Mary in disgust. "Mrs Drummond is doing a roaring trade, passing on information, and the Green looks like a Fair day."

"I thought things were quiet here," grimaced Alison. "No one's rung the doorbell all afternoon."

"Well, there it goes now," said Mary. "I'll answer it. I suspect that you are about to be drawn into the witches' porridge-pot." She hurried from the room, and there was the murmur of voices from the front door. In a few seconds, she returned.

"Alison, Kelvin's not back yet, is he?"

"No," replied Alison. "He went to visit the Taggards, and then I believe he had to make some other parish calls."

Mary Witherspoon disappeared, and the mumbling continued for some time at the front door.

When she came back she held a leaflet in her hand. She said: "That was Cynthia Chubb. She wants to see Kelvin.

She says she wishes to make Confession." Mary scowled. "I told her there were no Romans here."

"Mary. How unkind. She just wants a quiet word with the rector, that's all. My father doesn't mind. It helps her, I think. And it's harmless."

"A waste of time."

"Possibly. But that is what he's here for, after all, to ease tormented souls. Where is she now?"

"In the church."

"That's all right, then. I'll tell my father when he gets back."

"She's already seen him once this morning, after Communion. In fact, she's for ever dogging his steps and whining to him. She's growing worse, you know Alison. Her wits have addled. Kelvin had better watch himself."

"I think he's going to suggest a psychiatrist."

"A brain surgeon might be more appropriate," retorted Mary Witherspoon.

Alison protested: "There's no real harm in her. Her heart is solid gold."

"It's just her brain that's soft ... Oh, my God, what is she up to now?" Mary leaped through the kitchen door into the back garden, followed more sedately by Alison.

Miss Chubb was flying across the lawn towards them, wild eyed.

"It is the vengeance of the Lord!" cried Miss Chubb. Dramatically, she flung an arm in the direction of the church. "The vengeance of the Lord!"

Mary Witherspoon traced the path of the pointing finger with her eyes.

"It's a tree," she said blightingly.

Cynthia Chubb gibbered on for a while longer, then, still incoherent, grabbed her bicycle from the rectory wall, and raced off down the drive.

"She'll break her neck one day," said Mary.

Alison stared after the retreating figure. "What on earth was she talking about?"

"God knows, because I don't. And I haven't the energy to work at it. She grows worse by the hour. If she's not down on her knees in church, or distributing tracts, she's pedalling around trying to kill herself with toadstools ... Or pestering Kelvin."

"I'm sure he doesn't mind."

"No," said Mary Witherspoon, "I will say that for Kelvin. He may be abrupt and even downright rude to some of his parishioners – the strong, healthy, virile ones, like Stephen – but he's kindness itself to those who are bereaved, or weak, or suffering, or, like Cynthia Chubb, not quite right in the head. That's Christian charity for you."

There was, however, little evidence of kindness or Christian charity in Kelvin Hunter when he strode in, less than twenty minutes later. He had about him an impression of fury leashed in only precariously. His face was white, the muscles of cheek and jaw tensed, nostrils pinched. And when he spoke, his voice was shaking with anger.

"Would you believe it, some damned vandals have wrecked the churchyard!"

Alison and Mary stared at him, speechless.

"I said," he repeated, "that vandals have been into the churchyard and wrecked the place. Sergeant Leach is having a look round now ... Did neither of you hear or see anything?"

"No," said Mary. "And we'd hardly be likely to, would we? It's quite a distance away, and there's a thick laurel hedge all round. The churchyard can't be seen from the downstairs rooms, anyway, and unless the villains used a sledge hammer we wouldn't hear a sound. Did they break any of the headstones?"

Hunter shook his head. "Toppled one or two, and dislodged some of the kerbstones. But most of the damage is more nuisance value – sheer devilment – vases turned upside down and emptied, granite chips removed from the graves and strewn around, crosses tipped over, plants uprooted – that sort of thing."

Mary brought her hand down on to the table. "Miss Chubb."

Hunter stared at her.

Mary said: "That's what she must have meant, a while ago, when she came shrieking through here."

"Cynthia Chubb is certainly not the culprit," said the rector. "Some of those stones take a heck of a lot of muscle-power to shift them."

"No, but she had evidently seen the havoc."

Alison found her voice. "But who would do such a thing?"

"You tell me!"

"The Taggards?" hazarded Mary.

The rector scowled. "No. That's another thing. The Taggards' cottage was attacked, too. They were inveigled away by a message – purporting to come from Ellery Sugden, only it turned out that he knew nothing about it – inviting them to collect some surplus goods from Sugden Court. Well, you know what the Taggards are like, they'd never miss such an opportunity. Anyhow, while they were away their place was –" Hunter paused, considering. "Tossed, I think, is the correct jargon, and everything they own was smashed." His face tightened even further, setting into a mask. "The village is turning into a madhouse. Let us hope this is the end."

But it was not the end.

That night, just after three o'clock in the small hours, Alison woke with a start. Though the room was dark, it was not a total blackness and there was light enough to see the outlines of the furniture. She wondered what it was that had woken her. Everything seemed still. But, surely, there must have been something, some alien sound that had roused her? She sat up. Then it came again, slight, but quite clearly, the clink of stone on stone.

Not waiting to switch on the light or to pull on a dressing-gown, Alison shot across the floor to the window and looked across towards the churchyard. There was no moon, but clear and beautiful starlight, and the sleeping daisies showed up plainly on the rectory lawn. The church and its environs, however, lay in the shadow of the trees, hidden, and darkly brooding.

And there it was again. That faint chink of stone against stone.

Her eyes ranged the blackness beyond the trees. She waited, motionless, for long minutes. Nothing. Nothing but the deep, unstirring night velvet. She was just about to turn away, when she spotted the light, small and moving; a golden glow-worm that seemed to be gliding between the gravestones.

Someone was in the churchyard.

The vandals had evidently come back to finish their work of the day before.

It was not fear that Alison felt, then, but anger. She flew across the room towards the door, still not waiting to put on light or dressing-gown. Her fingers were round the handle of the door when she heard another sound, nearer this time, and instantly recognizable. Footsteps, very soft ones, in the hall, and then the scrape of a drawer. Snatching up a heavy, silver-backed hand-mirror from the dressing-table for a weapon, Alison quietly opened her door and tiptoed to the head of the stairs.

There were no lights on downstairs, but, in the glimmering greyness, she could see a dark figure stooped over the hallstand.

Viciously, she clicked on the light.

Kelvin Hunter spun round, dropping the torch he had been taking from the drawer. He stared up at Alison, blinking. For several heartbeats he did not move, did not speak, just stood like a man dazed.

Alison was looking enchantingly pretty in a long white nightgown, very simple, a curve across breasts and hips, her hair tumbling loosely down over her shoulders. There was colour in her cheeks and her eyes were brilliant with anger.

As she came towards him, Hunter stepped forward as if in a dream, his arms outstretched.

"Louise," he said.

"Father!" Alison's voice jerked him back to reality, and his arms swung to his side. He stood very still. "Father, I thought you were a burglar." She trod the last stair. "Did you see the light in the churchyard?"

"Yes." His cheek-muscles moved slightly. "I didn't want to wake you. I was going to investigate." He stood like stone.

"So, wait for Sergeant Leach." Alison's hand groped for the telephone.

And then Hunter did move. In two strides he was at her side and had gripped her wrist, forcing down the receiver.

"No, Alison, no. I wish to deal with this myself. There's no need to bring in the whole panoply of the law: this may be merely a couple of misguided teenagers – hoodlums, I grant you – but I can talk to them ..."

Unconvinced, Alison relinquished the telephone and stared up at him, her mouth curving into an unwilling smile.

She said: "Do you have to play Knight Templar?"

"Go and put something on or you'll catch cold," he said, in a curiously flat voice. "And wait here." Then, before she realised what he was going to do, he bent his head and kissed her full on the mouth.

An instant later, grabbing up the heavy torch, he strode to the door, opened it, and went out.

But Alison had never been very good at taking orders, and, pausing only long enough to slip into a coat and shoes, and to exchange the hand-mirror for a more lethal-looking poker, she followed her father outside.

He had already disappeared from the rectory garden, she could see his torch – for he had switched it on prior to entering the deeper recesses of the churchyard – a yellow circle on the ground, bobbing through the lychgate.

Without hesitation, she flew across the lawn after him. The grass was damp beneath her feet, the dew heavy on the tightly-budded daisies. Around her, hung the scent from a thousand night-dim roses and honeysuckle flowers. She carried no light with her, but the stars burned brightly, lighting her way and drawing sleeping shadows from the trees.

The rector had progressed to the most ancient part of the graveyard, Alison could still see his torch, a firefly among the black hulks of the old tombs. Here, where twisted yews crowded the gravestones, the pathways were tunnels of gloom.

Hunter's torch curved in a wide arc, curved back again. Bushes, headstones, crooked crosses, sprung into relief, then were gone again, swallowed into the darkness. A silent wind blew a shadow across the stars, and the trees in the graveyard shivered. A shade by one of the tombstones rose, like Lazarus, with lifted arms.

Alison was several paces from her father when the shadow leaped at him out of the blackness. There was a faint flurry of sound as Kelvin Hunter was struck very hard from behind. He crumpled where he stood, pitching forward to hit his head with a little crack on the plinth of a marble cross. The torch shattered beside him. Even as he fell, the bushes rustled and his assailant vanished into the night.

Alison made her way slowly forward, peering in front of her. She was almost upon her father before she found him, huddled in the long grasses beside the gravestone. He made no movement. She went down on her knees beside him, cradling his head across her lap. Through his hair, at the back she could feel the wet stickiness of blood, but she had no idea how badly he was hurt. There was another wound, a large lump, on his forehead.

She lifted her eyes, and her breath rasped in sharply with fear. There was someone standing in the shadow of the nearest yew tree, watching her. She caught the shine of eyes in the stray starlight. Gently, she began to push her father's head from her knees so that she could rise but, before she had completed half her action, the vague shape detached itself from the blackness under the yew, and went past her like an arrow, moving easily, in a long sprint towards the lychgate. The figure melted through, and was gone. And Alison and her father were once more alone under the staring stars.

Seven

Stephen opened his eyes to daylight, a dazzling morning light shafting across the room and striking daggers from the glass and metal fitments. For a moment, he struggled against consciousness, then relinquished the fight and lifted himself from his pillow. Aware that his head ached, and that his mouth felt parched and rough, he staggered over to the mirror and looked at himself with distaste: a white, haggard face sporting a stubbled chin and eyes bleary from drug-induced sleep. With none too steady hands he took his razor and attempted to subdue the bristles. Finally, he had several cups of strong coffee.

Today, he recalled, was the day on which he was supposed to collect Alison and take her into Redeham to catch the noon coach. Beyond that, he did not trouble to delve; it was painful to think, and so he did not try.

Half an hour later, he wandered into the garden for a few reviving breaths of fresh air to put himself into a more suitable condition for the journey – and stared. His car was in an even less suitable condition than he was – for this journey, or any other. It was standing on the gravel in front of his cottage on four very flat tyres.

Stephen goggled at it in disbelief. It had been perfectly all right the night before. Stepping across and bending down, he realized that the tyres were not only flat but completely ruined. They had been slashed with a knife, or some other sharp instrument.

His first instinct was to blame the Taggards, and then he

remembered that they were not there, their cottage was empty. The whole family was being accommodated at the Red Lion until the chaos the vandals had inflicted the day before had been dealt with. Ellery Sugden had kindly promised a gift of furniture and bedding, and others in the village had rallied round with offers of help. But none of the promises had yet materialized. Miss James and her lady helpers were coming that afternoon to repair the worst of the damage. Stephen had seen the mess: utter confusion, with furniture splintered, bedding slashed, china broken, and even Dixon's little clay animals pounded into powder underfoot. To Stephen, that had somehow seemed the greatest violation of all.

He stooped again and peered at his tyres and, as he did so, a large black car glided round the bend towards him. It stopped, and the driver, a heavy-featured, heavily-built man, leaned out of the window and queried: "Mr Brand?"

Stephen straightened and nodded.

The car door opened and the driver eased himself out, followed closely by the man who had been sitting in the passenger seat.

Stephen stared at them both, puzzled.

"I'm afraid," said the fat man, "that you're wanted at the rectory, immediately. There's some kind of emergency, I gather, from the young lady."

"From Alison Hunter? What kind of emergency?"

The second man, who was tall and thin, and whom his companion addressed as Dillman, said smoothly: "I'm sorry, we have no idea. She just said to tell you that there's been an accident, and she needs you – at once. We were coming this way, you see, and offered our help."

"OK" said Stephen. "Thanks. I'll be there as soon as I can." He bent again to his car.

Dillman moved towards him. "I see you have trouble."

"You might say that."

The green eyes held Stephen's. "The young lady really was most insistent that you should come at once. We'll run

you down to the Green, if you like. Be pleased to give you a
helping hand."

"That's very kind of you," said Stephen in relief. He
turned. "I'll just collect a few things."

A hand came down on his shoulder. "We must hurry, Mr
Brand, the young lady was in a terrible state."

"Alison? In a panic?" Bells began to chime in Stephen's
brain. The whole thing was beginning to sound decidedly
odd. Besides, though he possessed a disposition that was
rarely ruffled, he did not like being railroaded. He shook off
the hand.

"OK, then," he said. "You carry on, and I'll make my
own way to the village." Bending, he picked up the trowel
Rosalind had been using the morning before, and balanced
it in his hand. He turned towards his door. "I'll be as quick
as I can."

"We would prefer you to come with us now." The fat
man blocked his way.

Stephen's brows lifted slightly, and something flickered
behind his eyes. He said evenly: "I'm afraid you must
excuse me." He sidestepped the fat man, and Dillman's
long, thin fingers snaked out and caught his arm.

"But I must insist," said Dillman.

"Like hell you will!" Stephen knocked the hand from his
sleeve and carried on his way, but, before he could reach
the cottage, something hard pressed against his spine.

"Keep very still," said Dillman. "Very still indeed. This
is a gun I have in my hand and, if you make me nervous
with any sudden movement, it just might go off."

Stephen obeyed him because there seemed nothing else
to do. He stood like a statue.

"Put your trowel on the grass."

Obviously it was not going to be much use to him as a
weapon, so Stephen placed it at his feet.

"Now," said Dillman, "turn around and walk slowly
towards the car."

That, too, Stephen did without argument, having caught

a glimpse of the automatic pistol staring at him with all the malevolence of an evil black eye.

"I suppose I have the two of you to thank for that?" he said bitterly, nodding at the slashed tyres of his car as he went past.

"Just walk!"

"Who the devil are you?" demanded Stephen.

"That hardly concerns you, at the moment," said Dillman. "Get in."

Stephen paused, his hand on the black car's door. "Where are we going? What do you want?"

"You'll see soon enough. Don't ask so many questions."

"If this is some kind of joke –"

"Oh, I assure you, Mr Brand, it's no joke." The light green eyes had a staring, unpleasant intensity.

"I'll be missed," said Stephen. "My fiancée will be waiting for me; I made arrangements to pick her up this morning."

Dillman laughed, an ugly little laugh. "She's got a long wait, then."

"She'll wonder where I am. She won't be able to catch her coach."

"We must all make our little sacrifices," said Dillman. "Now, get in!" The gun ground its message against Stephen's spine.

"All right, all *right*, I'm getting!" Stephen stepped forward, slid into position in the back seat with Dillman and the gun beside him, and tried to look as harmless and peaceable as possible.

"Make sure the cottage is locked, Whooms," called Dillman to the fat man, who hurried up the path to slam Stephen's door before heaving his bulk into the driving seat of the car. He started the engine, and the vehicle moved forward smoothly, swinging into the first of the bends that corkscrewed along the narrow lane.

Within five minutes, Stephen realized where they were heading, and it was not to the rectory – although he had

never really believed that it would be. They had purred
away from Ardinford and then swung in a wide arc, and
were now travelling along the back road of the Sugden
estate. Gradually, the car slowed, swerved to the left, and
shot down the narrow spur of pitted track which led to the
chalk quarry, and to nowhere else. They bumped on for a
few minutes longer before taking the even dustier, narrower
track that descended to the quarry floor itself.

"Get out," said Dillman tersely, when they came to a
halt.

Stephen did as he was told, and looked about him. He
had been in the quarry only once before, and it had not
impressed him then as a place to linger. It impressed him
still less so, now.

Around him rose the quarry walls, steep and
unclimbable, with only one way out – the way they had
entered. This track, bare and composed of hammered
chalk, swooped down from the top of the quarry, curved
round in front of two wooden huts – some distance apart
from each other and with their backs to the rear quarry wall
– and then came to a dead end by an ancient chalk-fall,
which was covered in long, coarse grass. This extended in a
ramp behind him, making a pathway sloping upwards,
continuing, covered in grass and budding ragwort, and
overgrown with hawthorn bushes, until it joined the main
track, about two-thirds of the way up. A pool of oil-
scummed water had collected against the lowest part of the
chalk ramp, where the floor of the quarry dipped unevenly.
Several shallow archways, cut into the chalk cliff, housed
various pieces of equipment; storm-lanterns, and picks and
shovels and buckets, a few drums of tar or diesel fuel, and
heaps of coloured gravel.

As he stood there, with the sun beating down on his bare
head, and the dazzle from the white chalk surfaces nearly
blinding him, a third man emerged from the hut nearest the
main track descent, and came across to them.

"I see you got him, then," he said. "Any trouble?" He

stared at Stephen, and Stephen glowered back, measuringly. This one he could take on, any time. No gun, and no taller or weightier than he was himself.

"No trouble." Dillman showed his teeth. "Did you expect any, Hoat?"

"With you, one always expects trouble ... Has he said anything yet?"

"No, but he will," said Dillman ominously. "Is Ferris around?"

"No, he's not back yet. You'd better tie up our friend, here, and put him in the other hut."

Stephen suddenly galvanized himself into action, heeled back savagely at Dillman's leg, leaped forward and hurtled towards the car.

He had taken only two strides when the world seemed to split in half as he went down under Hoat's flying tackle, hitting his head on chalk that felt as unyielding as granite. For a second, he lay dazed, with the quarry spinning around him and no breath left in his body.

Hoat stood up. And Stephen felt he might have misjudged that particular adversary.

Whooms came forward then, and kicked him hard in the ribs. "Get up, slug, before I finish you." He aimed another kick as encouragement, and Stephen rolled sideways and rose unsteadily to his feet.

"Try that again," said Dillman, "and you'll trip on a bullet."

"What the hell do you want?" demanded Stephen, his voice thick.

"The diamonds," said Dillman smoothly. "All of them."

"Diamonds?" Stephen's yelp of surprise was not feigned. "I don't know anything about any diamonds."

The pistol barrel came down across Stephen's cheek. "Naughty, naughty!" chided Dillman. "You're not going to like what you see in the mirror if you persist in being so stupid—"

"I think you're all off your rockers," yelled Stephen.

"You must all be bloody mad!"

The pistol caught him again, knocking him sideways and making his teeth rattle.

"Leave him, Dillman," cautioned Hoat. "The boss will be back soon."

"I'm aiming to save Ferris some trouble," said Dillman. He turned again to Stephen. "Where are the diamonds from the briefcase — and don't say 'What briefcase?' because I mean the one you carried into the shop yesterday, empty."

"I never saw any diamonds," said Stephen. "The briefcase was empty." He jerked violently backwards as the pistol made its hurtful journey towards him again.

"Liar," said Dillman pleasantly. "The little girl thought we'd swallow lies, too, but she learned differently, in the end ... As you will."

"I don't —" began Stephen, then shouted: "You caught Rosalind, you mean? ... Did you? What did you do to her? Did you push her into the stream?"

"No —"

"Did you hurt her?"

"Only until she told us what we wished to know. And she admitted that her brother had hidden the stuff in the churchyard. Unfortunately, she gave us the slip before we could find out exactly where."

Stephen was staring at him, eyes in flames. "You Goddamned — You ... broke ... her ... fingers!" He no longer cared about the threat from the gun, or the unequal odds. He no longer cared about anything except taking that thin throat in his grasp and squeezing, squeezing, until all the breath was gone. He launched himself at Dillman, murder in his eyes.

Dillman tottered backwards and went down on to the ground under the onslaught. His gun slithered harmlessly across the chalk.

It took the combined efforts of Hoat and Whooms to prise Stephen's hands from his opponent's windpipe, and to drag him forcibly away. Dillman crawled to one side, wheezing, then picked up his gun and hit Stephen savagely across the back of the head.

When Stephen came to, he found that he was trussed as securely as a chicken, and that Dillman was lounging near him, watching him and smiling, those green eyes as cold and hard as glass. As soon as Dillman was satisfied that Stephen was fully conscious, he leaned over, hauled him to his feet, and propped him against the wall of the chalk ramp. Then, still smiling, he brought up a far from gentle knee and caught Stephen full in the groin.

Stephen doubled over, gasping.

"And that," said Dillman, "is a mere sample of what I can do. I can work it so you'd be no use to that pretty little darling you go about with ... Remember that, if you're ever tempted to tangle with me again."

Stephen unclamped his teeth from his lip.

"You're very big," he said, "with unarmed men and little children."

"I carry out my orders," said Dillman, bending forward and strapping a filthy gag across Stephen's mouth. "There ... Not because I'm afraid anyone will hear you, but because I'm sick of the sound of your voice. That will keep you quiet until Ferris arrives." And he thrust Stephen down on the ground and left him lying there, his face pressed into a dusty clump of ragwort.

Eight

Alison glanced at her watch, then out of the window for the tenth time in less than an hour. It was early, not quite mid-morning, and there was no reason at all why she should expect Stephen to arrive yet. But she was hoping against hope that he would.

As he was not on the telephone, and as no one had been available to send with a message to his isolated cottage, there had been no way of communicating with him, and she had been unable to let him know about her father's injury. Still, she had wondered if the grapevine, in its usual efficient fashion, might have somehow apprised him of the disaster.

Glancing out of the window again, she saw Miss James and Miss Chubb, together, wending their way along the drive towards her. Miss Chubb was pushing her bicycle and crying: Miss James was giving the support of her tongue.

Alison opened the door before they could ring the bell.

"Oh, my dear," gasped Miss James, "we've just heard about the attack on our poor dear rector."

"Oh?" said Alison.

Cynthia Chubb began to sob more copiously, and Miss James removed the bicycle forcibly from her hands and propped it against the rectory wall, catching a tendril of climbing rose as she did so, and pulling it away from its anchorage. For a moment, she struggled to repair the damage.

"That's all right," said Alison at last. "Leave it. I'll fix it later."

Miss James giggled. "Clumsy me ... Miss Chubb was on her way to see the rector when she passed me, and I was able to give her the news," she explained, with undisguised relish. "I told her" – she stared hard at her watery companion – "that she wouldn't be able to talk to Mr Hunter today. And maybe not for weeks to come. I heard all about it from Mrs Drummond, who'd seen the doctor –" Miss James paused for breath, but not much. "Such villainy. And in Ardinford, too. Whatever is the world coming to? A gang of teenagers wasn't it? – and the poor dear rector beaten up in his own churchyard."

"I think the whole thing has been highly exaggerated," put in Alison. "There was only one assailant, and one blow, and my father isn't badly hurt." She took Miss Chubb's arm. "Please don't cry, Miss Chubb, the rector is in no danger, he will be home again with us all, either this afternoon, or tomorrow. He was only kept in hospital for observation, and to check on the results of the X-rays." She added, with reluctance: "Won't you both come in and have some coffee?"

"Oh, no, thank you," said Miss James. "I just called to see if there was anything I could do. I'm on my way to Redeham, if I can catch the bus – it's my library day."

Mary Witherspoon came through the hall in her hat and coat.

"Then you'd better turn round and gallop back down that drive," she said. "You've precisely seven minutes to spare before the bus leaves the Green." She grasped Miss James by the elbow. "I'm coming with you. I've some books to change, and I want to call in at the hospital and see Kelvin."

Miss James craned her neck and glimpsed Alison's suitcase in the hall.

"I don't suppose you will be going to see your cousin, now?" she mourned.

2

BUSINESS REPLY SERVICE
Licence No CN 81

Keyhole Crime Books,
P.O. Box 236,
Thornton Road,
CROYDON,
Surrey CR9 9EL

Mary Witherspoon glared at her. "I fail to see why not. The rectory is in good hands and Alison's father would be the last one to wish her to spoil her holiday."

Miss James said: "And you are sure there's nothing I can do, Alison?"

"Quite sure, thank you. But it's very kind of you to ask."

Mary Witherspoon said grimly: "From now on in, Kelvin is going to be killed with kindness by his lady parishioners. They've only been waiting for an excuse to coddle him to death. You'll see. We'll be awash with soup for the next six weeks."

"Soup?" said Miss James doubtfully. "Do you really think the rector would like some soup?"

"Oh, Lord, give me patience!" cried Mary Witherspoon. "Lydia James, you're not as daft as you seem, are you? It just comes out that way ... Come on."

Miss James, being used to the caustic tongue of the older woman, took no offence and allowed herself to be propelled away from the door. As they both started off down the long stretch of driveway, a Land-Rover passed them and hooted a greeting before skidding to a halt beside the still snuffling Miss Chubb. The driver of the vehicle climbed out and limped stiffly up to Alison.

"Good morning, ladies."

Alison smiled. "Hello, Ellery. Am I to understand from this visit that you've already heard about the attack on my father?"

"Bad news flies, so they say." He grinned down at her, the scars on the dark face disappearing for a moment in the wrinkles of his smile. "He's all right, isn't he?" He stared at Miss Chubb, who was mopping herself with a large handkerchief. "Cheer up, Cynthia. You can always say an extra prayer for him."

"My father is fine," said Alison. "He'll be back home by tomorrow. Will you come in and have a cup of coffee?"

"No, thank you, Alison, I guess you have your hands full. I only came to see if there was anything I could do ... I've sent a couple of my men round to tidy up the churchyard. They're waiting for a special piece of machinery, at the moment, so there's not much they can do on the car park, anyway."

"Oh, thank you," said Alison, with real warmth at last. "That's most kind c´ you. My father will be delighted."

"And you, Alison?" His eyes were gently mocking.

"Of course," she said evenly. "That goes without saying."

Ellery Sugden stared down at her, no longer smiling, and Alison thought how little she understood him. She had known him since she was a child, been fond of him as long, yet still he remained a closed book to her. A deep, intense man whose motives were his own, and who acted always with set purpose. A man, too, who would hold a grudge. She did not delude herself that anything he did, now, was out of any affection for her.

"Remember, my dear," he said, "the cherry orchard is yours, for your Brownies, if you want it." He turned. "Chin up, Miss Chubb." He raised a hand in salute to them both, limped back to his Land-Rover, and was gone.

Miss Chubb continued to stare along the deserted drive long after the vehicle had disappeared. She was weeping again, the tears sliding down her cheeks in unchecked runnels. She looked as if she had not slept for a week.

She said, in a choked voice: "I will repay, saith the Lord."

"Yes, Miss Chubb, I'm sure —" Alison said, helplessly. "Oh, please, Miss Chubb, do come in and have a cup of coffee, or ... Brandy?" she hazarded. "Do, please, come in and have something. You'll make yourself ill."

"Later ... Later," said Miss Chubb in an abstracted manner. "First I must —" She walked unsteadily away from Alison, weaving slowly in the direction of the churchyard. Alison ran after her and caught her arm.

"Miss Chubb —" she pleaded.

The older woman turned and gave her a misty smile.

"Later, my dear. Later, there will be all the time in the world. I wish to go into church, first ..." She walked on, leaving Alison stranded at the edge of the lawn.

It must have been well over an hour before Alison again remembered Miss Chubb. Having been kept busy answering the door to well-intentioned callers, reassuring everyone that everything was well with the rector, and sorting through the ever-growing pile of articles destined for the Taggards, sifting the rubbish from the utter rubbish, Alison had had little breathing space. Now, she recalled her distressed visitor of earlier that morning.

At first she imagined that Miss Chubb must have already gone home, but, on checking, she found that the old bicycle was still leaning against the rectory wall. Several leaflets had blown from the basket. Religious tracts. Alison stooped to pick them up.

Undecided, she waited a few minutes longer, gazing across at the churchyard, then she stepped out into the garden and hurried across the sun-flecked grass to the lychgate. As she walked down the path to the church she caught sight of a young man with white curly hair working assiduously over one of the far gravestones. Hearing her step, he looked up and briefly raised a hand to her before going back to his task of tidying the grave.

Alison entered the church by the west door, leaving it open so that the sunlight cut a golden swathe along the centre aisle. The interior of the building was dim after the brightness outside, the grey walls soaring upwards into shadow on either side of her. The church was a tiny place with nave and chancel only, and it took but a quick glance to assure Alison that Miss Chubb was not in any of the pews.

She walked slowly up the aisle towards the altar, above which the lovely stained glass window glowed with coloured light, scattering jewelled cascades of amber and emerald, ruby and amethyst, across the cool stone floor.

There was the scent of lilies in the air.

And something, some alien thing, upon the altar.

Alison approached and picked it up. She recognized it, or, at least, she knew exactly what it was, and who had made it. It was one of Dixon Taggard's little clay animals. A cat with glass eyes.

There was a scrap of paper where it had stood – the crumpled fly-leaf from a hymnal. Alison smoothed it out.

She stood looking down at Miss Chubb's spidery handwriting for a very long time, while a whole world of misery passed before her eyes.

I know, now, that in this life there can be no forgiveness for such as I, and perhaps I am doing only what should have been done twenty years ago. Because of what happened then, two children died – two children are dead again. Accidents both, they say. Yet fingers point, tongues wag ... But if one is guilty, then all are guilty. In this thing.

And I do not know what to do.

True, I did talk to Dixon Taggard on the afternoon of his death, about lunchtime, and I lied about that: I gave him some sweets, and he gave me the little clay cat you will find on the altar. I think he liked me – a little. And I was there that evening, on the Leap, but by then the child was already dead, I saw his broken body at the foot of the cliff, and I had nothing to do with that, I swear. My sin was – and is – in silence, nothing more. But that can be a grievous sin.

C.C.

Alison finished reading Cynthia Chubb's agonized letter, and found that her eyes were starred with tears. Who ever knew what slept inside the flesh? She went quickly back down the aisle to the west door, and paused in sunshine. Then, very slowly, she back-traced a few steps and put out her hand to the vestry door. One twitch of the iron latch, and she had pushed it open.

Miss Chubb's square-rimmed glasses lay on the vestry table, a wooden chair was up-ended on the floor. Miss Chubb herself was hanging by the neck from the central beam, haltered with her own leather belt, her body revolving heavily in the draught from the door. Her face was swollen and distorted, blue, her eyes bulged grotesquely. But whatever had once tormented Cynthia Chubb, would torment her no longer.

Time slowed to a crawl as Alison stood there, motionless. For an eternity of seconds, she closed her eyes. When she opened them again, she realized that her body was trembling uncontrollably; her mouth, dry. In a daze, she reached out and placed the clay cat and the letter on the vestry table.

There was nothing else she could do there.

Forcing her leaden feet through the door, she closed it, and turned the key in the lock behind her.

When, eventually, the statements had been made and the questions had ceased, when the doctor and the policemen and the photographers had completed their work, and Miss Chubb's body had been removed, Alison, at long last, remembered Stephen.

The clock said three-thirty. She looked at it again, frowning in disbelief. But there was no mistake. It was three-thirty in the afternoon, and Stephen had not yet arrived. Not that it mattered. She had no intention of going to stay with Veronica, now. Both her father and Mary Witherspoon would probably assure her that the day's events need make no change in her plans — Mary, especially, with her insistence that Alison should invite Stephen to go with her so that they could have some time on their own together — but she could not leave her father now, not even for a few days. If Stephen needed her, then Kelvin needed her, too, and perhaps his need was the greater.

Trailing into the hall, Alison picked up the telephone.

Veronica seemed strangely unsurprised that the visit was cancelled, and Alison felt too exhausted to query her cousin's odd comment that she was "glad you are holidaying with Stephen."

"I'll write to you," said Alison. "And explain everything, and make other arrangements." Because, of course, she thought drearily, there would be a post mortem, and an inquest, later.

"See you at the wedding," said Veronica, with a little laugh.

Alison unpacked her case, and refilled it with articles for the Taggards. When Stephen arrived they could run it up to the cottage. She looked at the clock again. Where was Stephen? He had never let her down before.

She lugged the case out on to the step, and looked along the drive. No Stephen. But Miss James was puffing towards her.

"Hello, Alison," she greeted her. "I've just come off the bus. Mary Witherspoon asked me to drop these library books in, on my way home. She's gone on to the hospital." She glanced at Alison's suitcase. "I intended to leave them on the step, because I didn't think you'd still be here." Miraculously, the news of Miss Chubb's death had not yet penetrated as far as Miss James. Alison did nothing to enlighten her.

"Did you see any sign of Stephen's car in the village?" she queried.

Miss James stared at her. "No. But the fishman from Redeham was by the Green when I got off the bus, and I happened to mention that I was going to those cottages this afternoon, and he said he'd just come from them, and that there was no one up there at all. Stephen's car is still there, though, with flat tyres."

"Then I expect he's walking – taking the short cut." But Alison was still puzzled. It didn't take nearly four hours to cover the distance, even if he had not discovered the faulty tyres until almost midday.

"Yes," said Miss James cheerfully. "I must hurry, Alison, I'm going to have a bite to eat, then several of us have planned to clean the Taggards' cottage. Captain Sugden has promised to run us up there in his truck, along with some furniture."

"How nice," said Alison dryly.

When Miss James had gone, Alison stood, still undecided, on the step. Then, suddenly making up her mind, she picked up the case and headed for the churchyard and the meadows beyond. If Stephen had no transport and was no longer at his cottage, then he must be taking the short cut. There was no other explanation. She would meet him half way, and they could snatch a breathing space together. Besides, she would be expected to do her share of operation clean-up! And, on the practical side, Stephen would be able to carry the case to the Taggards.

It was the case which, in the end, proved to be the difficulty. It was heavy, and bulky, and the day was hot, and by the time Alison had walked more than half way along the lonely track towards the cottages, Stephen had still not materialized. She decided to dump the case, for the moment; Stephen could collect it later. She looked around. Wildness on every side. On her left, there was a swaying stretch of uncut grasses, rosy with sorrel and spires of timothy, and, beyond that, a barrier of bushes; blackthorn and hawthorn and threading trails of green-flowering bryony. And here and there a seedling birch. A perfect hiding-place.

Alison struggled forward and pushed the suitcase behind a hawthorn, then stood up, and flexed her aching shoulders. On the other side of the bushes, she knew, was the chalk quarry, plunging in a sheer drop a hundred feet or more. No sound came from below. Presumably the workmen were toiling on Ellery's new road. There was the thin crack of a gunshot, far away, from the direction of the south wood. Nothing else. Around her, only a sea of insect humming and the scent from sun-baked grasses.

Alison still resented the high-handed way in which Ellery Sugden had closed her Brownie pack's usual camping ground, with little notice, and bare apology – and for his own ends. Surely, with the whole of the estate to choose from, his workmen could have been based elsewhere?

Impulsively, she thrust her way between the screening bushes until she was poised on the lip of the quarry, looking down. There did not appear to be much there in the way of heavy machinery, though, to be fair, that was probably all up at the working site. Although Ellery had offered accommodation at Sugden Court, she imagined the huts in the quarry were being used for eating and sleeping and recreation purposes, for a couple of men were lounging on the grass slope in front of the wooden buildings ...

There was no time to see or consider anything further. A thick arm shot out and wrapped itself around her waist, jerking her violently backwards among the bushes.

"Well, now," said a voice, "what have we here?"

Before Alison could scream, a hand clapped brutally over her mouth.

"Just keep that pretty mouth closed." said the same voice, "or I shall have to close it for you."

As the hand slid away, Alison turned her head. Her captor was a heavily built man in his twenties, and he was holding her very tightly, in a grip that was more bear-hug than embrace.

"Let me go," she gasped. "You're crushing my ribs."

She felt the bone-cracking pressure relax slightly, and promptly repaid that Samaritan gesture by clawing at his face with the nails of her free hand. As he cursed and involuntarily raised a protecting arm, relaxing his hold on her waist even further, she wriggled from his grasp and started to run. He lunged after her, but she was light on her feet, and desperation gave her wings. In ten seconds, she was already outpacing him. But she didn't get far. A few strides along the overgrown track, and another man appeared out of nowhere, arms spread, cutting her off. She swerved, but this second opponent flung himself forward and she went down with him on top of her, pinned to the rough grass. He rammed her arms to the ground with his own so that she was helpless, gasping, the apricot-scent of agrimony foliage heavy in her nostrils.

"Get her up, Hoat," said the voice of the man she had clawed.

The weight was taken from her back, And Alison rolled over and sat up, still gasping.

"It's Brand's girl, the rector's daughter," said the man called Hoat. "What do you think you're up to? What are we going to do with her?"

"She was prying into the quarry, and she might have spotted Brand" said the fat man, holding a handkerchief to his injured face. He brought it away from his cheek covered in blood and looked at it for a few seconds, then at Alison. "You shouldn't have done that to me," he said softly. He glanced across at his companion. "Anyhow, the boss said we were to keep intruders away as things might start moving at any moment ... We could throw her over the edge, make out she's had an accident."

"There have been too many accidents," said Hoat.

"Yes," said the fat man, smiling nastily. "And it would be rather a waste. There are better things we can do with her." He raked Alison insolently with his eyes, and leaned forward to put a hand on the curve of her breast.

Alison kept quite still, realizing that any show of resistance would bring both those huge hands crawling over her.

"Leave her alone, Whooms," said the other man. "We can't kidnap half Ardinford."

"Well, we certainly can't let her go."

Hoat looked at Alison. "We'd better get her to Ferris." He brightened. "Perhaps the sight of her will loosen Brand's tongue a little. And Ferris can decide what to do with them both, afterwards."

"Are you mad?" whispered Alison.

Whooms jerked her to her feet. "Shut your mouth or someone'll shut it for you."

Hoat took a pistol from his pocket. "That's right, lady, do as you're told before you get hurt."

"I don't believe this," said Alison. "I just don't believe it.

This is Ardinford, not Sin City."

"Come on, lady," said Hoat. "Behind those bushes there's a passable way along the top of the quarry. We go to our right, and round, until we meet the main track leading down. OK? I'm sure you know where I mean. Now – move!" He gestured with his gun.

But Alison was still feeling argumentative.

"You wouldn't dare use that thing," she said.

Hoat came very close to her, and pressed his gun just behind her ear. "I don't like smart ladies," he said, very softly. "Would you care to try your luck?"

Alison backed down for the moment, and they made their way along, and down into the chalk quarry, walking quickly if, on Alison's part, with more than a little inner rebellion. But there was nobody here to help her. She would have to bide her time.

"There you are, Dillman," said Whooms, pushing Alison forward so roughly that she stumbled and almost fell, "there's another to add to your collection."

Dillman rose and shook out his lanky length and stared at Alison. He began to smile – a white-toothed, animal smile. And Alison knew then, quite certainly, that she had run out of road.

Slowly, he reached out a hand for her, a narrow, slender hand, with the fingers of a musician or an artist or, Alison shuddered, the kind of fingers one could imagine might belong to a strangler. Stepping backwards, she half-turned. And then she saw him. Stephen. He was lying on the sloping ramp beside them, half hidden in the long grass.

Alison took a jerky little breath, unable even to call his name.

He lay motionless, staring at her over the filthy gag, his eyes slate-grey in the sunlight, with a kind of blaze in their depths. He was covered with chalk and dried blood, and he was still bleeding from a gash on the head. He had been beaten and he had been bruised. But at least he was alive.

Alison flung off Dillman's restraining hand and flew

across to her tightly bound fiancé.

Dillman pulled her back against him, holding her almost caressingly. She kicked him, dragged herself free, and returned to Stephen.

Dillman came at her again, the white, animal smile once more on his face.

"So you fight, do you, my pretty," he laughed. "The harder they fight, the sweeter they fall." He cuffed her across the side of the head.

Hoat said, warningly: "Ferris will want a word with her."

"Don't worry," purred Dillman. "I may not hand her over intact, but providing she can move her mouth ..."

Alison picked up a chunk of chalk and hit him with it, hard, in the teeth.

And Dillman lost what little control he had left. He said thickly: "I'll tame you, my beauty, if it's the last thing I do ... Whooms, grab her legs."

Alison, who had never in her life, until that day, had an ungentle hand laid upon her, didn't like the experience, and whirled on them like a wild-cat, kicking and biting and scratching. She was deaf to threats, oblivious to hurts. Reason had flown from the coop.

Stephen struggled against his bonds, unable to speak, unable to make her understand. Every movement she made against them was making things ten times worse for herself. And he wondered if she realized what they would do to her. He clenched his fists impotently as they hauled her away from him.

Ripping the cloth of her blouse with violent fingers, wrenching her hair from its anchor pins, they dragged her roughly to the first of the wooden huts, which stood in the welcome shadow of a wing of rock.

Stephen was sick at heart, half-mad with rage – and totally helpless.

And then the screaming began, high and agonized. Screams that went on and on and on ...

Nine

It was some time before Stephen realized that the screaming had stopped.

Gradually, he became aware that he could hear a grasshopper in the weeds beside him, and the small pattering of falling chalk, and, somewhere high above, larks singing. He slowly opened his eyes. He had clenched his lids, clenched his hands, clenched every muscle in his impotent body, so it seemed, against inner pain and the acceptance of what was happening, and now the sun swam before his eyes in a red mist that was as much bloodlust as physical hurts or dazzle.

Quite simply, he wanted to kill.

There was the pattering of chalk again, to one side and a little above him, and, raising his head, he saw a man swinging down the track towards him. The newcomer stopped short, a few paces from Stephen, and looked around, frowning. Then he leaped from the ramp, which was about shoulder-height at that point, and headed along the quarry floor to the first and largest of the huts.

No great powers of deduction were needed to tell Stephen that this stranger was the missing Ferris – the boss. He had an air of authority and sharp decisiveness that immediately singled him out as a man who would lead rather than be led. A man who would stand no nonsense. He was of medium height and build, with a strong nose and jaw, dark, straight eyebrows and thick dark hair. His eyes, too, were very dark, of that obsidian quality which reveals little of inner thought.

He was obviously less than pleased with his underlings.

"What the devil's going on?" he shouted as he reached the door of the hut. "Where is everybody? There's no guard on the quarry, no one helping Curly in the churchyard, no one doing damn-all, as far as I can see – and Brand tied up in full view of anyone who likes to wander down here ... What the bloody hell do you think you're up to?"

He disappeared into the hut and, a few minutes later, his men trooped out before him in various stages of disarray, looking sheepish, cowed, or deflated, according to temperament. Even the swaggering Dillman retained all the *panache* of a pricked balloon. Stephen noticed with satisfaction that the mark of the rock was still on his mouth.

Ferris's dark face held such a blaze of anger as to make him almost unrecognizable.

"When I give orders, I expect them to be carried out – to the letter. Is that clear? With no improvisations, no foul-ups, and no added frills which you feel might make things more entertaining. Is that clear!"

His men shuffled and mumbled.

"My God, I'm surrounded by incompetents," went on Ferris savagely. "I can't leave you to do the simplest thing, without you bungling it in some way or another. Not only do you allow a child to lift a fortune from under your combined noses when I depart for five minutes, but you can't even search a churchyard at dead of night without arousing the whole neighbourhood. And now I find you fooling around with some girl –"

"We had to bring her here," said Dillman sullenly. "She was spying on us. She's Brand's girl, the rector's daughter."

"I know who she is!" spat Ferris. "And I'll overlook the gross inefficiency that allowed the girl to approach the quarry in the first place, but I will not tolerate the kind of sloppy behaviour which puts this whole project in danger. Is that clear! We are here to do a job, quietly, and that job is going to be done ..." His voice dropped to a menacing purr. "With or without you."

The men shuffled their feet.

"Well, we know you said no booze and no women," said Dillman, still truculent. "But this was different, wasn't it? It was pickings. We didn't think it could do any harm, and it would have been a waste to —"

Ferris cut in coldly: "If there are any pickings to be had, I'll be the one to have them, not you. And don't you forget it. Now, get about your business." He turned. "Whooms, take a rifle and remain here. I want you on guard outside the huts. Over there, on the lowest section of the ramp should do ... Hoat, collect another rifle and guard the top entrance into the quarry. The transaction is to take place here — at any time — and we can afford no more eye-witnesses. I don't want anyone down here unless you first check with me. You can signal from where you stand." He swung round on Dillman. "And you, my fine randy friend, can help to find those stones. You can remove yourself to the churchyard and turn yourself into a lawnmower ..."

When Ferris was satisfied that his orders were being obeyed, he strode across to Stephen and ripped off the gag.

"Now," he said. "We can have a little talk."

Stephen glared up at him, wishing his mind were as numb as his wrists and ankles.

"Alison," he said thickly. "Is she all right?"

Ferris stared at him with those dark eyes which showed nothing of the mind within. "That," he said, "seems a singularly stupid question."

"I'd like to smash you all," said Stephen.

"I can well believe that. However, it is a desire that will have to be shelved, for the moment." Ferris paused. "Now, may I have your version of the briefcase story? We learned from the Taggard child that she had spoken about it with you, and with no one else, fortunately — not even her parents."

"Go to hell," said Stephen.

"Not just yet, Mr Brand ... I know, of course, most of what happened, and why. I wish to check your side of it, that is all."

"Why should I tell you anything?"

"Why, indeed? But the position has altered slightly: you have now the girl to concern you. If you are stupid –"

"All right. All right. I'll tell you what I know, for what it's worth," said Stephen. And he proceeded to relate Dixon's story of the briefcase, as Rosalind had reported it to him.

"Yes," said Ferris. "That is what I thought."

"Then it was a bit pointless bringing me here, wasn't it?" snapped Stephen.

"Not at all, Mr Brand. I would not like to think of you spreading your story around. You have not done so, have you, Mr Brand?" His voice was deadly quiet.

"I think you know exactly what I said to Mrs Drummond," answered Stephen. "Just that we'd found the briefcase, and that was all."

"Good, good." Ferris's smile flickered. "Anyhow, I wanted to have a word with you myself – I never trust second-hand information. Unfortunately, my men are more enthusiastic than tactful, and I imagine they must somehow have aroused your suspicions; I regret that our little chat must be held in such uncomfortable circumstances."

"And you would have let me go, after our – little chat?" enquired Stephen cynically.

"Now, Mr Brand, you can't really believe that I would be so foolish? No, of course you would not have been allowed to go. But you would have been housed with as little discomfort as possible, I assure you."

"And now," said Stephen, "you are going to kill us both?"

Ferris laughed. "You have the strangest notions, Mr Brand. I don't knock off tiny people. What danger do you think you and the girl are to me? No one has missed you; in the village, everyone thinks Alison Hunter has gone to see her cousin, and taken you with her."

"And when her cousin phones to ask where we are?"

Ferris shrugged his shoulders. "If she does that, gossip will merely say that you've gone off for a few dirty days together. It happens all the time. Even with a rector's daughter."

"You've got it all worked out."

"I try," smiled Ferris, "I try ... You will, of course, remain here until we leave, but that shouldn't be too long, now, and if you behave yourself you will have no further cause to regret our company. Your sojourn with us, Mr Brand, can be reasonably comfortable, or it can be most unpleasant, it is quite up to you –" Again he gave that flickering smile. "I trust you will be able to console Miss Hunter ..." He jerked his head in the direction of the first hut where Alison was standing in the doorway, holding tightly to the door-post.

Once she realized that they had spotted her, she came slowly across to them, swaying slightly as she walked. She could barely stand upright, but Stephen saw at once that this was no weeping, hysterical woman they had to deal with. Her mouth looked bruised, her face white, and her hair was hanging in long, loose, untidy curls over the torn blouse. She looked battered and shocked and, incredibly, very desirable. But whatever her hurts, whatever her feelings, she had ridden them out and clamped down upon them. Only her eyes betrayed her, their cool ash-grey deepened into a smoky blue. Stephen noticed that Ferris had stiffened and was watching her with rapt attention.

She said, and her voice was as unsteady as her feet: "Stephen, he can't let us go when he leaves, whatever he says. We've seen them all, we could recognize them again, give descriptions – And he is the ringleader ..."

Ferris said coolly: "This is neither the place of my birth, nor the country of my adoption. I do not think, Miss Hunter, that I have a great deal to fear from you."

"If that is so," she said, "then untie him," She nodded towards Stephen. "He's been trussed up like that for hours. His hands and feet are terribly swollen."

"It might teach him to keep them to himself," said Ferris imperturbably.

Alison's lips quivered. "Please untie him."

"And why should I do that?" Ferris leaned towards her.

"For humanity's sake, if nothing more."

He smiled down at her. "Tied like that, he can do no mischief. You see, already he seems to have damaged several of my men ..."

"They've damaged us, too," said Alison, in a low voice. "I think you could afford to call it even."

"Mr Brand, here, threatens to 'smash' us all, should he get the chance – and overlooking the fact that I could tackle him with one hand behind my back."

"I've got two behind mine," gritted Stephen. "What's stopping you?"

Ferris stepped forward and dealt him a blow across the face that took Stephen's breath away.

Ferris said pleasantly: "I deal in violence, but I am not a violent man, Mr Brand. There are two things only which make me angry: stupidity, such as you have just shown, and disloyalty. My men are frequently stupid, they are *never* disloyal – twice."

He wound one of his hands in the silver waterfall of Alison's hair and jerked her head back, still keeping his eyes on Stephen. "And, believe me, it is very stupid to try to be smart when you have none of the advantages and the opposition holds your hostage." He jerked at Alison's hair again, so that she gasped and cried out. "Just be thankful that it is I who am here, and not one of my men. They are less tolerant than I. And, next time, think before you speak."

He released Alison's hair, and her head shot up. She said nothing at all, but stared at him with stormy eyes in a kind of dumb hostility.

"I'm sorry about that, my dear, but it was a necessary little demonstration if we are all to get along together. It is essential to convince you both that defiance is dangerous ... Now, I shall question your story again, Mr Brand, and remember that I already know a great deal from the Taggard child. I wish to see if what you have to say tallies with her tale: make sure that it does."

Again Stephen repeated the story as far as he knew it.

Ferris said: "And the child never made it clear where the diamonds had been hidden?"

"No. I told you. I didn't even know they were diamonds. Dix merely told his sister that he'd got rid of the rubbish in the duster."

"Rubbish? Very valuable rubbish, Mr Brand. A fortune in uncut diamonds. Close on half a million pounds' worth."

Uncut diamonds! Stones without sparkle, looking like pieces of sea-washed glass. But rubbish, none the less, thought Stephen, to the small child who already possessed a vast quantity of broken windscreen glass.

Stephen shot him a look. "How can you be so certain that the diamonds were in the briefcase when Dix stole it? You yourself had left the car. It seems to me there would have been ample opportunity for your men to substitute something else for the stones – the chase with the boy could have been a cover-up, especially when he was found so conveniently dead."

Ferris snapped: "That is out of the question. They know better than to double-cross me!" Contempt curved his mouth. "Besides, the diamonds must have been in the child's hands, how else do you explain this? We took this from his sister." He felt in his pocket and drew forth a small clay horse, broken now, but still recognizable. It was Rosalind's horse, the one she had carried with her in her shoulder-bag. Stephen realized, now, what had been missing when he found the bag beside the river.

Ferris said: "The eyes are diamonds."

Stephen stared at him in disbelief. "They can't be."

"I assure you, they are."

"Then –" Stephen looked puzzled.

"You have something to add, Mr Brand?"

"No, not really ... Anyhow, it doesn't make sense. But if the eyes in that horse are diamonds, what about the rest, the eyes in Dix's menagerie of clay animals which you crushed when you turned over the Taggards' cottage? You couldn't have overlooked them." He was still puzzled. Surely, all those had been made by the child long before the briefcase was stolen?

Ferris stared at him with dislike. "Let us not play games, Mr Brand. They were glass, as you very well know ... I am not asking for anything to which I am not entitled, I am merely trying, very patiently, to retrieve something that is mine."

Alison put in, glacially: "Then why don't you go to the police?"

The dark eyes held hers. "There are – certain difficulties in pursuing that particular path."

"You mean the diamonds are stolen property!"

"No, not at all. but there are – certain reasons why my organization does not wish anyone to know we have such a quantity of uncut stones in our possession. We are here to buy certain ... things." A smile touched the corners of his thin mouth. "It is a transaction of which the authorities might not approve." He nodded. "We have been granted a few days' extension by the dealer, because of our ... difficulties, but, after that, the – objects – we desire will be offered elsewhere. So, you see why we must regain our property? And soon?"

Stephen said: "Then it might have served you better to have been more gentle with Dix; a bag of sweets and a soft word would have brought you all you wished to know."

"No one regrets that accident more than I do, Mr Brand. As you say, a soft word ... But my men were too enthusiastic in carrying out my orders, I am afraid, and frightened the child –"

"And his sister," said Stephen nastily, "did their enthusiasm also frighten her to her death?"

"You are a cynic, Mr Brand. But, yes, the little girl's death was the last thing I wanted: she had not told us all we wished to know."

"She didn't *know* anything," said Stephen hotly.

"She had spoken with her brother."

"And he'd told her he'd thrown the diamonds – the rubbish — in the churchyard."

Ferris smiled grimly. "Down among the dead men."

"What?"

"Those are the words she said her brother used," explained Ferris. "He said he'd thrown the stuff down among the dead men."

"But she didn't know where?"

"She didn't tell us where," Ferris corrected gently.

"It's a chant," put in Alison.

Both the men turned their heads to look at her, and Ferris raised his brows.

"Down among the dead men," repeated Alison. "It's a chant, a children's singing game. Dix used to join in with the Brownies – oh, he wasn't supposed to, but he did, and I couldn't see any harm in it, the poor child had little enough fun in his life: I had no objection to him being an honorary Brownie – and that was one of our games. You know, pow! wow! He used to play it by himself, sometimes."

Ferris stared at her as if she had gone mad.

Alison tried to elucidate. "You dance around a make-believe totem pole," she said. "Pow! wow!"

Ferris looked even more bewildered.

"Red Indians!" Alison said helplessly. "But that makes no sense at all, does it – not with your lost diamonds?"

"And you have one of these – totem poles?"

"No, of course not," said Alison. "We just use anything near at hand –".

"Then it appears we'd be more sensible to continue with our original intention of combing the churchyard – if you have no better ideas." His voice was sarcastic.

Alison shook her head. Catching Stephen's gaze on her, she took a step closer to the ramp and stretched out an arm. She laid her hand, very lightly, against his cheek, and smiled. And her eyes stared down at him with love. If he had ever doubted her true feelings for him, he had little cause to doubt them now, for her heart was looking out at him.

"Very touching," said Ferris dryly.

"Can't you untie him?" pleaded Alison. "His hands are swelling. He'll be crippled for life if you leave him like that ... We'll do anything you ask."

Ferris looked at her with a strange expression in his eyes.

"You are in no position to bargain," he said.

"Please, let me untie him." She bent forward, and he watched for several seconds, an amused smile on his lips, while she struggled with her fingers to undo the tight cords that bound Stephen's wrists. Eventually, Ferris caught her shoulders and pulled her back towards him. For a moment he stood, with his arms wrapped around her, then slowly turned her to face him. He still kept her pinioned, his length pressed upon her, and he could feel her heart beating wildly against him. It was a long time since he had desired a girl so fast and so intensely.

"You are good at striking bargains, are you?" he queried. "Well, we shall see."

"I don't think —" began Alison.

"You don't?" His voice was gently mocking.

"What do you want?" Alison whispered. But she already knew what he wanted; it was herself, wasn't it? And there was no real choice. Ferris or —? All Ferris had to do was to leave Stephen tied up tightly. Stephen might not die, but ... alive could also mean not quite dead.

"I see we understand each other," said Ferris, half smiling, his eyes on her face. He took out a pocket-knife, opened it, and held it towards her, the point between her breasts. "A bargain?"

She nodded.

"No, Alison —" cried Stephen, working impotently against his bonds. He felt sweat start on his body.

Ferris turned on him coldly.

"Mr Brand, you are well aware that I could take your girl whether she is willing or not. That I do not do so, is because I find little pleasure in coercion. That should relieve you ... I see that it does not."

"If you harm her —"

"I haven't the slightest intention of harming her. She might even enjoy it."

"If you harm her —" began Stephen again.

Ferris was suddenly very still. "If I harm her, you will do — what? Mr Brand. Really! Your threats are infantile. Obviously, you do not fully understand the situation here." He reached out and pulled Alison to him again, and she stood unresisting while he undid the remaining buttons on her blouse. "In this place," said Ferris, "I am God. I hold the power of life and death, of pleasure and pain — and I can break you any time I choose. Please remember that, Mr Brand ... You are very fortunate that I believe your story. This is a week in which I have been sorely goaded. Do not try me further, for I have small patience with people such as yourself, who are conditioned to easy living and privilege." His voice was as hard as glass. "I have a group of men here, who are just within my control, I do not aim to let that control slip. They work for me because they are paid, and paid well, to do so. To a great extent, I impose my will upon them; I have the means, and I have the power. Unfortunately, they are often stupid, sometimes erratic. They see you as a threat, and the girl as a bonus — do you follow me? I am your bulwark, Mr Brand." He pulled aside the cloth of Alison's blouse and bent his head.

"One day," said Stephen, through clenched teeth, "I will kill you. I promise you that." He writhed forward.

The dark eyes lifted, chillingly, and Alison cried out: "No, Stephen, no! Stephen, forget it. It's all right. It doesn't matter. None of this matters. Stephen! Stephen! Don't rile him." She caught Ferris close in both her arms and held him, and saw Stephen shut his eyes in defeat – or pain.

Ferris said: "If a man wishes to keep a girl he should first make certain he is clever enough to hold her, and strong enough to protect her."

Stephen remained silent, eyes closed, riding out the taunt.

"Untie him," said Alison softly. "And perhaps he will show you."

"Really? Would he really? I wonder." Ferris's voice sounded tired. And, stooping, he sliced the cords which bound Stephen's wrists and ankles.

Stephen tried to push himself to his feet, and collapsed again where he had been lying. From frozen numbness, his limbs kicked themselves alive with wave after wave of paralysing pain, so that he felt himself gurgling in agony against his clenched teeth. But, gradually, the hurt of the free-flowing blood lessened and he recovered sufficiently to realize that Alison was crouched on the ramp beside him, massaging his swollen wrists, and that he must be cutting a far from heroic figure. Once more he tried to stand, and this time succeeded in remaining upright although he was still none too steady on his legs. He took a tentative step. Hurriedly, Alison gave him the support of her arm and shoulder, and he tottered forward along the ramp.

"Get down from there," said Ferris dictatorially.

They obeyed him as well as they were able, Stephen landing in an ungainly sprawl upon the ground. He was still showing all the agility of a sack of cement. Alison helped him to his feet.

"Go across with him to that second hut," Ferris commanded her. "I'll come for you later."

Lurching and swaying, they preceded him over the rough ground to the wooden storage hut beside the rock-fall. Once there, Ferris lifted a heavy bar from its sockets and flung open the door. He motioned them inside, then slammed and locked the door behind them. the bar thudded into place and they heard Ferris's footsteps receding towards the other hut.

Stephen sank down and began to rub his ankles into more active life, while Alison looked around. Really, there was nothing to see. The place was empty, save for a tarpaulin in one corner. Both windows of the hut were high and covered, on the outside, with wire-mesh. The building itself was strongly constructed of new wood. There were no loopholes, no gaping cracks, nothing that appeared to suggest any weakness at all. The floor consisted of sturdy, nailed boards; the door was locked and barred. With nothing but bare fingernails to work with, there was little chance of breaching either.

When Stephen had recovered his strength, he lifted Alison to each of the windows in turn. The front one stared over the main part of the quarry, facing the ramp, the sloping path, and Whooms, who was sitting on a tar-drum, reading a comic book. His rifle was propped beside him. The other window looked towards the first hut, which was built on much the same lines as the one they were in, except that it was larger, erected for living accommodation rather than storage, and sporting the more usual eye-level type of window, although none facing in their direction, only a waist-high, lidded bunker against the blank wall. The rear and remaining side wall of their prison were also blank.

There was no way out.

And it was late evening before anyone came near the prisoners again. Then, it was Ferris, crashing back the door and standing in front of them framed by the pale June dusk.

"Had you thought I'd forgotten our bargain?" he said, laughing down at Alison, his teeth a flash of whiteness in the gloom.

He held out his hand for her, and she went with him without a word.

Ten

The sun was already well up over the eastern edge of the quarry before Alison was returned to Stephen's hut next day.

There came the rattle of a key in the lock, the creak of wood, and then she stood in the doorway, holding a tray complete with sandwiches, a can of steaming tea, and a couple of chipped enamel mugs. Having had nothing to eat or drink since the previous morning, Stephen was relieved to find that they were not about to be starved to death.

Alison stepped into the bare room without speaking, avoiding Stephen's eyes, and the door slammed behind her. Once more they heard the key snap in the lock and the bar thud into its sockets.

Stephen said: "Was that Ferris?"

Alison shook her head. "Whooms. He's been detailed for guard duty outside the huts again." A faint smile. "The others have changed round, but he enjoys squatting on his tar-drum."

Stooping, she placed the tray on the floor beside the folded tarpaulin. "There, eat. I'll join you in a moment." She spoke jerkily, through stiff lips, and Stephen noticed that there were blue smudges beneath her eyes, and her face was pale, the fine skin drawn tightly over her cheekbones in strain, or sheer fatigue. Somehow, she had managed to have a wash, and her hair was tied back with a length of cord.

Her blouse was tied, too, at the centre-front where two buttons were missing, with another piece of cord. But instead of fulfilling the intended gesture towards modesty, it served only to give her a kind of raffish, decadent air that was singularly provocative. Stephen felt his body stirring in spite of himself, and he clamped down on his thoughts harshly. Oh, God, why now, when the last thing she needed was another pawing? Any show of affection, any attempt to take her into his arms, and she would probably recoil from him in revulsion. At the moment, her feelings were battened down, all reserves stretched, he dare not touch her and risk breaking that tightly-wound nerve.

"Are you all right?" he asked, recognizing the inadequacy of his words.

"Yes," she said, "yes," and continued to fiddle around with her sandal. Stephen could not tell what she was thinking. He knew so little about women that he was unable to put himself in her shoes. He had spent a sleepless, tortured night, picturing Ferris's body doing what it pleased with hers, and knowing that he himself was powerless to prevent it. With no tools of any kind, other than his bare hands – he found his pockets had been emptied – he was unable to do anything, either constructive or destructive, in the way of escape. His mind had gnawed round and round the events of the day before, chewing at this and that and considering means of breaking loose, but always it had returned to that – Alison and Ferris, together.

And he found himself stiff with rage.

"Did he hurt you?"

"No." Alison's face was shuttered.

Stephen slanted her a burning look. "We'll get out of this," he said, "and Ferris is going to answer for everything, that I promise you. In all that has happened, to us, to the children, the ultimate responsibility is his. His the fault, his the orders –"

"If we get out of it," said Alison. "Do you believe they will release us when they leave? I don't." She gave him her straight, grey-blue stare.

Stephen said honestly: "No. I don't think so, either. We

can identify them." He hesitated. "They'll probably keep us alive till they do go, though, in case they suddenly have need of a couple of hostages."

"You mean we have to rely on ourselves to escape from this place?"

"Yes. Unless the cavalry come riding to the rescue, and that seems pretty unlikely." He glanced upwards to the window.

Alison said slowly: "Everyone will believe that I've gone to Veronica's — except Veronica — even my suitcase has vanished. It's sitting under a bush at the top of the quarry."

"And they'll just assume that I've decided to go with you," added Stephen, his voice gloomy, "though my car is still outside the cottage. They'll imagine that we skipped across the fields to Redeham Halt to catch a train. No one is likely to miss us until school starts again, on Monday."

Alison stood up and walked across the floor to squint through a narrow crack they had discovered down one side of the door.

"Presuming we can find a way out of this hut, could we make it safely to the top of the quarry?" she asked.

Stephen joined her beneath the front window and placed his eye to the chink of light by the door-hinge.

After a while, he said: "I think I could deal with Whooms, there, on his tar-drum. Where he is now, sitting in the shade of those hawthorns, he can't be seen from the other building. He isn't too bright, and I'm sure I could creep up behind him, over the rock-fall. And that would give us his rifle. But after that —" He stared upwards. "The main track is in full view of the first hut, there's no way of pussyfooting up that unobserved. Even if we took the ramp path which curves out of sight behind those bushes, it still has to join the main track to take us from the quarry. They'd spot us from the hut and pick us off, then. Besides, as soon as they came out, shooting, the guard at the top would be down on us. We'd be caught between the two lines of fire."

"You really think they'd shoot at us then?"

"Oh, they'd shoot at us, all right," said Stephen bitterly. "I don't think they are equipped with rifles for fun."

Alison pondered. "Some kind of diversion?"

"It would seem so." He frowned. "Somehow, we must lure that guard at the top of the quarry down the main track so we can move in behind him from the ramp path ..." He turned his head. "Still, we have to find a way out of this prison, first."

Alison handed him a six-inch nail. "Is that any use? I slipped it into my sandal when I picked up the string for my hair ... There are lots of them lying around outside, all shapes and sizes, thrown down when the huts were erected, I suppose. I'll try to snatch another one, if I have the chance. I thought perhaps we could dig round the nail-heads in the floorboards with it. Loosen them, somehow, and make ourselves a bolt-hole." She considered. "It will have to be in the floor, so that we can hide our activities with the tarpaulin."

"Is there space enough underneath? Can you see from outside?"

"Yes. I checked. The huts are built up on cross-beams. It will be a tight squeeze, but fortunately neither of us is over-endowed with flesh." She flashed him a smile. "It should be possible to crawl through a hole in the floor – if we can make one – and then come out from under the hut."

"Then we'd better start our bolt-hole at the back, so that we emerge at the rear, beside the quarry face where we can't be seen. And after that –" He frowned again. After that would come even greater problems.

Stephen swept his eyes across the floor. The boards ran from side to side in varying lengths. He judged the right-hand corner, as he faced the rear of the hut, to be the best spot for his assault. The planking there was in shorter pieces, as if the workmen had been using up some offcuts. Heaping the tarpaulin at his side, so that it could be flicked across his excavations at a second's notice without causing any suspicion, he started work. He used the nail point to chisel away wood from around one of the nail-heads in the corner board, then put the free point under the exposed head, and levered.

It was a hard, slow business, levering back and forth and continually shifting the position of the six-inch nail with which he was working so that he could bear upon it equally from all sides. The sweat was soon streaming into his eyes, for the hut grew progressively hotter and more airless as the sun rose higher through the day, beating down mercilessly on their small wooden hell, and his fingers became raw and aching, and so stiffened that they would hardly hold his pitiful tool. But he kept on doggedly. Poke, slide, lever ... lever ... Alison helped him from time to time, but her wrists were not strong enough to make much impression on the nail-head, and she took over from him for short spells only when he was unable to continue any longer without a rest.

"It'll take weeks, at this rate," cried Alison in despair. "We'll never do it."

"The first fastening will be the worst," muttered Stephen, bending to his task. The nail-head in the flooring had moved slightly and he found he could wag it from side to side with his fingers. "After that, I should be able to lever from under the loosened section of the board —"

It was, indeed, a little easier, once they had removed the first nail from the floorboard, but not very much, and the nail they had prised forth proved to be useless as another tool as it was too bent and too short.

"Damn," said Alison in disgust, thrusting it beneath the tarpaulin.

Stephen said nothing, but lowered his head and put his aching fingers to work once more.

Twice, during the day, Alison was taken from the hut to make coffee and sandwiches for the men. On neither occasion was Ferris in evidence, but she was treated by those around, if not with respect, at least at arm's length, for she was Ferris's property, for the time being, and therefore untouchable. They did not, however, seem to care what conversations she heard, which augured ill for her future. And Dillman's leering eyes followed her around with disconcerting intensity: when the hour came, when Ferris no longer wanted her, she knew he would be waiting ...

After the second excursion, late afternoon, she returned to the prison-hut with a box of matches she had managed to purloin.

"There were several boxes lying around," she explained to Stephen, as she pulled the spoils from her blouse. "Three of the men smoke, and I was allowed to light the calor gas stove to heat the water for the coffee. There doesn't seem to be anything else there of any use, though – not that I can put my hands on, anyway. The cutlery is all plastic, and there's not even a bread-knife, it's ready-sliced bread."

She handed the box to Stephen. "There, keep it safe. We might be able to start a fire as a diversion, once we get out of here ... And I've discovered what we're all waiting around to buy. Arms."

Stephen stared at her.

"You know, armaments – guns," she elaborated. "They're taking out a consignment of guns. A lot from what I hear, and the latest kind – M.60s, or something, if that means anything to you."

"I should say so!" said Stephen. "That's about the most fiercely-desired machine gun there is. American, I think."

"Well, the transaction is supposed to take place here, in the quarry – their diamonds for the machine guns, when they arrive."

Stephen's face had a hard look. "How did you find out all this? You sound very chummy with our nasty friends."

"The men talk – they forget that I'm there."

"I doubt that very much," said Stephen grimly.

"Then I can only imagine they believe it can't matter, and that our final destination is to be a hidden grave on a dark night." Alison gave him a thin smile. "Where would they obtain arms? I mean, who would deal with them?"

"It could be someone with a consignment bought from an arms dealer on forged official documents, or –" He frowned, thinking back. "There was a big theft, a few months ago – it was in all the papers – a load of arms lifted from some lorries travelling to a nearby military base. I think there were M.60s in that lot. A full-scale hunt took place, but there were rumours that the stuff had been shipped out of the country. If I remember correctly, a cargo boat was held and searched at Gravesend, after a tip-off, but nothing was found. And then, a bit later, a couple of ships docked at Dublin were given a going-over. But that, too, turned out to be a false alarm. So far, there has been no confirmation of the arms being put to use anywhere – at least, not in those quantities."

"They could have been hidden, all this time?"

"It's possible. Get the heat off, then find a buyer at leisure."

"Would that be difficult?"

"You must be joking! Illegal organizations would cut each other's throats to obtain a consignment like that. Have you any idea of the damage all that hardware could do? In the wrong hands ... Terrorists –"

Alison looked at him in dismay.

Stephen said: "The problem would be removing the stuff across country."

"The road-working equipment. The heavy vehicles! People accept their presence without question."

"Yes," said Stephen. "It all looks innocent enough, doesn't it, trundling around from place to place? They might even have fixed themselves a perfectly legal contract for wherever they are aiming to deliver the goods."

"And that could be virtually anywhere in the world –"

"Yes. It could also be closer to home – Northern Ireland, for instance."

"They don't sound Irish," objected Alison.

"They don't have to hang out a placard."

There was a long silence, then Alison said slowly: "Ellery Sugden was in Ireland ... You don't think Ellery could knowingly be a party to all this, do you?"

Stephen jabbed at a nail. "I have no idea. He could be in it up to his neck, or they could just be using him as a cover. One thing, though – Ferris didn't take the diamonds with him when he arrived at Sugden Court that day. Do you remember? He left them in the car."

"And Ellery was injured by an IRA bomb. He'd hardly be helping those who maimed him."

"The IRA doesn't have a monopoly on violence," said Stephen dryly. "And Sugden might very well want revenge for his injuries. His life can't be easy –" He handed Alison the short length of board he had taken from the corner, and she slid it beneath the tarpaulin.

She said, with a certain satisfaction: "Anyhow, Ferris doesn't hold the diamonds now, so he can't pay for the arms."

"It's only a matter of time," said Stephen. He levered at another nail-head. "But if we could get out of here –" Another thought suddenly struck him. "Do you think Ferris will come for you tonight?"

"Yes." There was no point in pretending otherwise.

Stephen dropped the nail with which he had been working, and grabbed her arm.

"If I ever lay my hands on him – if I ever get him, man to man, equally, with no guns, and no back-up gang, I ... will ... kill ... him. I swear. Slowly."

Alison gave him a wan smile. "Of the whole bunch, it is Dillman who frightens me most."

"Dillman!" Stephen gave a contemptuous grunt, picked up the long nail, and applied himself to his task once more. "Dillman is merely a hired man. It is Ferris who gives the orders and is the one to watch. The leader. Ferris is the one to fear."

"For you, perhaps, said Alison. She looked at him oddly, and paused. "But, for me, Dillman is the very devil."

"And Ferris is not?" Stephen's voice was quiet.

Alison realized how much he had changed in a few short hours. There was something haggard about his bruised face, and the lazy, gentle manner had gone, perhaps never to return. The Stephen she had known and loved, who would never willingly have harmed a fly, was contemplating, quite cold-bloodedly, the most extreme form of violence against another man. Not merely contemplating it as some means to an end, either, but as vengeance and — she frowned — with something like enjoyment.

She regarded him from under her lashes. "While Ferris holds his claim on me, the others leave me alone."

"And we are to thank him for that?" said Stephen, his eyes snapping. "The bloody hell we will!"

"Stephen, believe me, things could be so much worse."

He turned on her, burningly. "Could they? Could they, really? You forced by Ferris, and nothing I can do to stop him?"

Alison looked at him for a long moment. She passed the tip of her tongue over her lips. She wanted to reassure him that she was safe, that Ferris was not a monster. But how? How could she explain that a practised man could take a woman against her will and still bring her to acceptance?

"He did not ... hurt me," she said at last. "He was ... very kind." She saw, too late, that it was the wrong thing to say.

"Perhaps it's easier for you to go, than it is for me to remain here, waiting and wondering," said Stephen, in a deadly tone. "Yes, perhaps it's easier for you."

Alison lifted her eyes which were as cold as glass. "Yes, perhaps it is," she said, and he understood what an unforgivable thing he had said.

"Oh, hell, hell, *hell*! Alison, I'm sorry —" He touched her hair. "If you knew how useless I feel —" He turned back to the hole in the floor and wrenched savagely at a piece of boarding.

"Will you finish the bolt-hole tonight?" she asked, her voice steady.

"I doubt it," he looked down morosely at the narrow strip of uncovered floor. A slight breeze blew up through the gap and fanned his arm. "Besides" – he read her mind – "when we go, we go together." Ferris could be allowed no revenge on a helpless captive.

Stephen levered at a loosened nail-head, although he could hardly see what he was doing. Inside the hut it was now almost dark. Beyond the windows the sky had deepened to a violet blue in which hung the glittering eyelash of a moon. Starlight. Night ...

He thought on Ferris with hatred. And wrenched at the boarding again.

Eleven

Alison opened her eyes. Morning. Sky as blue as a dunnock's egg, and sunshine. A heartless, golden sunshine streaming down from the cloudless sky. That much she could see, and no more, through the dusty window above her. She turned her head. No vivid, erotic dream, then, but reality; the man's dark hair still beside her, rumpled in sunlight, his face showing less harsh in sleep, the skin bluish along the jawline with a night's growth of beard.

She eased herself up against the pillow, afraid to move lest she should wake him, and looked around. It was a squalid little room, with its tumbled sheets on linked cots, its bare boards, its plastic spoons and tin cups and shelf of filthy dog-eared paperbacked books. Piles of girly-magazines and comic papers heaped the floor, which was strewn with cigarette butts ground out carelessly against the boards. There was a stove, a table, and four folding chairs, one of which was covered in clothes; his clothes and hers – her skirt, her blouse, both just showing from beneath his chalk-plastered shirt. Her brief panties had slipped to the floor. She stared at them blindly. After a few seconds' hesitation, she stretched out an arm, groping, but was unable to reach the chair.

She eased herself further up the pillow and leaned forward across the sleeping man at her side. Still, she was an arm's length away from her goal. Her breath went out on a little sigh of frustration. Drawing her legs up smoothly beneath her, she bent forward again. But her efforts were useless. Either she had to remain where she was, naked, until he woke, or she had to scramble from the bed and rouse him for certain. She debated the two evils, then glanced down again to find that he was already awake, his dark eyes staring up at her. There was a faint smile on the thin mouth.

"Problems?" he laughed softly, as she shrank away from him against the wall.

He sat up, still keeping his eyes on her. There was a hot glimmer in their darkness. Unable to move any further from him, Alison continued to stare at him as if she were hypnotized, saying nothing, but he could see that her breath was coming in short, rapid bursts from between her half-closed lips, her breasts rising and falling in tantalizing rhythm.

Abruptly, his hand shot out and round her, pressing firmly in the hollow of her back, thrusting her towards him. Her skin was cool and taut, smooth beneath his fingers. Beautiful.

He had wanted her from the first moment he had laid eyes on her, had known he would take her, for there was no one to stand in his way, but, that done, he still wanted her. And there was the difference. Lust was predictable, he had set out quite cold-bloodedly, and almost mechanically, to arouse her and bring her to acceptance of him, arrogantly certain that her senses would be unable to hold out against him. A sexual awakening, he had thought with cynicism, for which she should be grateful ... But rape? Hardly! His lips twisted. He despised any show of force in bed, for, in the end, there was no such thing as an unwilling woman – only an impatient man. And he recalled the sweet June night.

But, somehow, he had become infected with his own poison: there was something about her that continued to heat him, like a fever in the blood. Uncharacteristically, he found his thoughts turning on her even when she was not by his side. It was uncharacteristic – and dangerous.

Ferris caught Alison's eyes still on him, remote and lost; those strange eyes that were sometimes one colour, sometimes another; sea-grey, sea-blue, a mermaid's eyes. She had this cool little way of looking at him that drove him mad ...

He caressed her lightly with his free hand, and felt her quiver under his fingers, swaying forward almost imperceptibly as if drawn to him by a magnet.

His body was fast moving out of his control. And there was no time for this; there were things he should be doing, people he should see. He should be up and about, organizing affairs, going places – Yes, lust was predictable, but this was something else again. Inexplicable. Surprising. A wild attraction of two identities. She was the only girl he had ever met who was able to stand between him and what he knew he should be doing ... And was she such an innocent victim?

His finger traced a slow, deliberate line from her neck down to her navel.

"Do you hate me?" he murmured, feeling her silk beneath his hand.

She moistened her lips. And his questing finger traced its path again, warm and relentless against her flesh, on and down ...

She shuddered against him.

"No." He answered for her. "By God, you don't!"

And he knew, now, that he could not help himself, could not help the stirring in his blood or the hardening of desire. Sure of her submission, he knew the whole world could go hang for as long as it took to possess her. What he should be doing no longer mattered, only what he did –

She came to him without resistance, her eyes large and drugged-looking on his, her lips slightly parted. She surprised him, but, then, she had surprised him from the very beginning. The freshness of her, and the fire. The participation that he was able to call forth, delightfully, and quite deliberately, even against her will, and under it all, that coolness, as if she waited, watching, and – also quite deliberately – stood outside herself while her body met his in passion. Until the very end ...

And then when at last he took her, it was not meekly in surrender, but as kindling to his flame.

Ferris surfaced, he knew not how much later, aware that all was not as it should be. A slight, cold breeze was blowing through the hut, raising the hairs on his thighs and driving ticklish little paths across his bare flesh. He rolled on to one elbow and lifted his head, then gave vent to one loud, harsh obscenity.

Ellery Sugden was standing in the open doorway, watching them.

Grabbing for his trousers, Ferris was in them, zipped, and standing up, in one smooth co-ordinated movement, and he walked across to Sugden whilst buckling his belt.

"Can't you bloody well knock?" he said, still furious.

"I've been knocking for the last five minutes," said Sugden blandly. "But neither of you would have heard the trump of doom." He looked past Ferris to the bed, where Alison had jerked upright and was now sitting, rigid, facing him, her hair tumbled about her bare shoulders. And, for the first time, he realized who this girl was.

"Christ!" he said. "What's she doing here?"

"I should have thought that was pretty obvious," said Ferris dryly.

"You mean – No! I don't believe it. She'd never be here of her own free will. Do you know who she is? She's Alison Hunter. She's the rector's daughter."

"So everyone keeps informing me."

"Then what the devil do you think you're playing at?"

Ferris told him.

He told him why she was there, and when, and how, and when he had finished Sugden still wore a scowl like thunder.

"You'll have to get rid of her. Now! At once! It's far too

dangerous to hold her here. If she got back to the village –"

"She's going nowhere."

"You'll have to kill her when you leave here, anyway, so it might as well be now ... If you're endangering everything just so that you can have a quick grapple when you feel like it –"

"Shut your mouth!" said Ferris savagely. "It's no concern of yours. Brand's here, too."

"My God! Who's entertaining him?"

Ferris's eyes snapped. "He's quite secure."

"I hope so ... I think you must be mad." He surveyed Alison. "Not that she appears to be objecting, does she?"

He seemed unable to take his eyes off the girl, which was hardly surprising, thought Ferris sourly, as she was sitting there without a stitch on. He moved over to the bed and lifted the sheet around her shoulders. She trembled a little as he touched her.

Sugden grinned at him. "This would be one in the eye for our Reverend Hunter, if he knew. He has a kink about any man laying hands on his daughter – and, from what I've seen, Ferris, you've gone a whole lot further than that –"

"I doubt that you'll be rushing back to tell him."

"No. But if he ever found out, he'd hunt you to the ends of the earth and cut you into pieces, he's that kind of man. Implacable. And clever. And Alison is his one ewe-lamb. I've often suspected ..." He smiled nastily. "I study human nature. Most of it is rotten ... Anyhow, you can't keep her here, it's not safe. Neither can you allow her to go screaming back to the law –"

"What do you suggest?" Ferris's voice was quiet, dangerous.

"Get rid of her. Get rid of the pair of them, right now. Let them be found twenty miles away, dead – or, better still, not found at all. I live here, I intend to live here after you and your mob have gone, so I'm the one who is most at risk through this caper."

"If you are, then it's your own fault. There was no need for her to see you. No one asked you to come down here, slumming."

Sugden was brought back sharply to his reason for the visit.

"I had to come. I've had a telephone call from the dealer. He wishes to speak with you at ten o'clock this morning – on my phone. He'll ring through."

"Oh?" said Ferris.

"Something's turned up. He needs to speak with you." Sugden paused. "We've lost our contact, so you'd better make sure you're on that line at ten."

"That's all right with me," said Ferris. "I want him to hold things up a bit, until I'm ready to deal. I shall need another day, or so."

"Well, you're out of luck, then," said Sugden. "He's already here."

"Here! In the village?"

"I imagine so. Or nearby. That's what I came to tell you. There are to be no more delays. He's coming to see you himself, today, to finalize the deal."

"Hell! When?"

"That's what he wants to talk to you about. So make arrangements with your hound up there to let him through ..."

Ferris said: "What's he like? The dealer? A reasonable man?"

"I've no idea. I've never met him: we did all our business through a go-between."

"You spoke to him on the phone."

"I spoke to someone," corrected Sugden. "It could have been Uncle Dan the flower-pot man, for all I know."

"Oh, very droll –"

"Look, Ferris, I'm being paid to provide your cover and the quarry for the transfer. And that is all. A straightforward transaction. Or so I thought. By now, it should all have been over. I've stuck out my neck enough for you already. I'm not sure that I shouldn't have explained, right away, that your payment wasn't merely delayed but bloody well lost! Anyhow, from now on in, you're on your own. If you can't come up with something for the dealer today, then you'd better toddle off home and let him find another buyer."

"Like hell I will!" said Ferris explosively. "When I go, the guns go with me, you can be very sure of that."

Sugden looked uneasy. He said: "Ten o'clock, then?"

"OK" said Ferris. He strapped on his watch. "I'll come up to Sugden Court with you now." He turned to Alison. "Get dressed. You can stay in here, make some tea and sandwiches for Brand and the boys, clear the place up a bit –" He looked at her again. "Get dressed." Still she did not move. Just sat there, very straight, staring before her with huge, blind eyes.

Sugden spat: "You can't hold her here. You can't! Kill her now. If you won't, I will."

"You will not," said Ferris.

"Because you want your bit of fun while you're waiting," said Sugden in disgust. "What have you done? Promised her her freedom if she's a good little girl?" He stared across at Alison. "Well, he's lying about that, sweetie, however prettily you dance for him –"

Ferris cut in: "She and Brand might make useful hostages. You never know –"

"You wouldn't be so keen on preserving her if she looked like Whistler's Mother," snapped Sugden. "And when you go? What then? You can't take her with you, you know that. They'll both have to be disposed of then. There's no other way."

Ferris, following Sugden outside, knew that Sugden was right ... There was no way out of this one. He slammed the door behind them, and Alison heard the engine of the Land-Rover race to life. And then they were gone, whining up through the quarry.

They were back within the hour. Alison had opened the

door to allow fresh air to circulate in the stuffy little hut, and she saw the Land-Rover sweep down the main track and slew round between the two wooden buildings in a flurry of powdered chalk: Ellery always drove far too fast, kicking up dust: She heard the engine die and, the next moment, Ferris's voice calling to her, imperiously.

"Alison!"

Slowly, she went to the open door and stood there, gazing across at him.

Ellery Sugden had parked the Land-Rover just beyond the second hut, where the ground sloped up to the pile of fallen rock, and now he and Ferris were lounging beside the ramp, talking. Whooms was in his usual position up on the ramp, a short distance away from them, sitting in the shade of some hawthorn bushes. She could just see his canvas boot.

Catching sight of Alison, Ferris called her name again and beckoned her. He was holding something in his hand.

She went reluctantly towards him.

"There," he said smiling, and pushed the object he had been holding into her hand. "A present."

She stared at him and then at her hand, and saw that he had given her a peach. Ripe. Perfect.

"From Sugden's hot-house," he explained, still smiling down at her. "It was the best one I could find."

Alison stared again at the peach she was holding, then, very deliberately, stretched out her arm and dropped the fruit into the water beside them. It sank through the oily scum and disappeared. For a moment, Ferris watched the spreading ripples, then turned to her, black brows drawn.

"That was a bloody Tom-fool thing to do," he said, his voice thick. He caught her by the shoulders. And, for several heart-beats, Alison held his gaze with a small, thin smile that did not reach her eyes.

Dropping his hands abruptly, Ferris swung round on his heel without another word and strode across to the first hut. When he was almost at the door he wheeled, shouting:

"Whooms! Lock her up with Brand. There's the key. Catch!" The key came spinning towards the ramp, but fell short, landing in a little spurt of chalk dust. Ellery Sugden bent and retrieved it.

"It's all right," he called across to Whooms. "I've got it. I'll lock her in for you."

Whooms, who had risen to come forward, sank back on his drum and continued munching peanuts.

Once Sugden had taken Alison's arm, as if to escort her to the prison-hut, he muttered fiercely: "Alison, listen to me! Listen carefully, and don't interrupt, and don't look as if I'm saying anything to you of any importance. Bend down and buckle your shoe, or something."

Alison flung one quick sidelong glance up at him, paused fractionally, then bent forward, her hand on the strap of her sandal.

"Good," whispered Sugden. "Now, listen carefully. I'll try to get you out of this, you and Brand. But it's not going to be easy. You're going to have to trust me and do as I say without question."

Alison kept her head down and concentrated on her sandal. For a few seconds her fingers manipulated the buckle, then they crept out stealthily and circled a six-inch nail half-covered with the dust. She pulled it carefully towards her, made a neat thrust, and slid it safely alongside her foot by the lining of her sandal.

Ellery Sugden went on, not paying her any heed but gazing across to the quarry wall: "I'll try to leave your door unlocked now, and then decoy Whooms into the first hut for a while, with Ferris. After that, I'll make some kind of excuse to go to the truck, and that will give me chance to remove the bar from your door – I'm afraid I can't do that until I get rid of Whooms because he'd spot it was missing at once ... If I succeed, you and Brand must make your way to the Land-Rover and climb into the back and lie down under the rug there. Whatever you do, don't try anything until Whooms is safely out of view – give me ten minutes from the time I call him, to remove the bar and get him settled with Ferris. Right? The guard at the top can't see that part of the quarry, so he's no problem."

Alison said nothing, but straightened slowly. She stared at him stonily.

Sugden smiled at her, and whispered: "Relax." He leaned back against the ramp, his lame foot resting on a roll of fencing which had been coiled away from the water.

"I don't find it a relaxing situation," replied Alison. She stooped and picked up a short length of cord that littered the ground, and began to tie back her hair. "And you've changed your tune suddenly, haven't you? A short while ago, you were all for killing me out of hand."

He seized her arm. "I could hardly show lover-boy that I was interested in your welfare."

"Suppose Ferris had taken you up on your suggestion?"

"Well, he didn't, did he?" hissed Sugden, propelling her forward. "And, I promise, if I find it impossible to free you this morning, I'll be back for you both ... So, if Ferris comes for you again, keep your mouth shut." He sounded nervous. He was wearing a blue plaid shirt which was open at the neck and Alison could see a pulse throbbing in his throat.

She shot him an odd look. "About what?"

"All our little secrets." Yes. Unmistakably nervous. Alison contemplated her chalk-covered hands. "Things have changed," went on Sugden. "The dealer won't wait, Ferris can't pay — and Ferris wants those arms. Once he knows where they are, that will be the end of us — of you and I, and Brand. Because I am beginning to suspect that Ferris will cross the dealer, grab the lot, and run. So make sure you keep dumb until I get you out of here, no matter what happens. You mustn't let him guess that you know where the guns are hidden."

"That shouldn't be too difficult," returned Alison, with a sardonic lift to her brows.

Sugden gave her an uneasy smile. "Good. Play it cool. And don't forget, I'll be here to help you."

"I'll believe that when I see it, Ellery, dear." Her lashes swept upwards. "So you've had the armaments all the time? Was that what you were paid for, to be the warehouseman? And where? Up at the Court?" Would he, really, endanger his beloved home?

Sugden scowled at her as he lifted the bar from the door. "Don't be so foolish." He seemed about to add something but, in the end, thought better of it and remained silent. Stooping, he fiddled with the key in the lock and thrust open the door. "There. In you go, and remember what I said – ten minutes from the time Whooms goes into the hut before you go to the Land-Rover. Let me make sure he's occupied ... And keep yourselves well down and covered."

She glanced at him again, uncertain, her eyes shadowed, the breeze teasing a skein of her hair across his arm. His face looked strained, the scars that marred it standing out whitely against the tanned skin.

"Trust me, Alison," he whispered, as he pushed her inside the hut. He pulled the door closed, called to Whooms and waved, giving the fat man a thumbs-up sign as he swung away towards Ferris's hut. And, standing at the crack by the door-hinge, Alison watched him limp from view.

Twelve

"What was all that about?" queried Stephen, as he turned from the door. He was crouched by the tarpaulin, looking up at her. "That was Ellery Sugden, wasn't it? I thought he would be in on this with Ferris, somewhere." Peeling back the canvas, he revealed the hole on which he had been working. "Almost finished, now. It's taken longer than I expected because I hit up against a concrete support of some kind, and had to start again."

His voice was blank with weariness but betrayed nothing of the bitter disappointment he must have felt after most of his earlier work had gone for nought, and Alison could only guess at the sheer courage it must have taken to begin the labour all over again. She stared at his wrecked hands, barely recognizable now, with the blisters torn into raw, bleeding flesh and painfully embedded with spinters. And her heart lurched. His face looked hagridden under the stubbled beard, and she suspected he had slept but little during the night.

Stephen flicked a quick glance up at her. "Are you all right, love?"

She nodded, and remained staring down at the hole in the floor. She could feel a slight current of air.

"Ellery says he'll take us out, in his Land-Rover," she said quietly. "He says that he'll leave our door unlocked and get rid of Whooms."

"What!"

"Yes. Sounds a bit far-fetched, doesn't it? Especially as he's in this over his ears." And she went on to tell Stephen all that had happened since she had last seen him. "So, why should Ellery decide to help us now?" she concluded.

"Has he left the door unlocked?"

"I'm not sure. I can't tell by looking at it, and I daren't try the handle while Whooms is still out there, listening and watching. Anyhow the bar will have to be removed, we can't open the door with that in position." The clear eyes lifted to his. "And if Ellery does all he's promised, and more, I still don't trust him. The whole thing could be a trap. A way of forcing Ferris's hand. If we step out of here, are seen to be escaping —"

"Ferris will shoot us?" Stephen frowned in reflection. "It seems a lot of effort for Sugden to make, just to liquidate us a bit sooner." He smiled up at her. "Have you considered that he might still be a little in love with you? He was keen on you once, wasn't he?"

"Only on what I could bring him," said Alison shortly. "No, that isn't it. If anything, he bears a grudge for times past. Besides, if he rescues us, he puts himself in jeopardy, and he's not going to do that: I might talk, and you most certainly would. And we know he can't fly off to the other side of the world, and escape that way, because he would never relinquish Sugden Court. Never. The Court is Ellery's life. No, if he takes us out, he's going to kill us."

Stephen looked puzzled. "But why, then, go to all that trouble? Why not wait and let Ferris do it for him?"

"Perhaps he doesn't trust Ferris's judgement. Maybe he's afraid Ferris will let us go."

"Maybe."

Alison's eyes had a faraway look. "But Ellery was frightened — not about what I may do when I'm out, but what I could do, here and now. His main concern is to force me away from Ferris before I can talk. But about what? About the hiding-place for the guns? He seems convinced that I must know where those guns are. But I don't." She turned. "I don't."

"What exactly did he say? Go over it again, see if it gives you any clue."

"I've been over it in my mind, again and again. Why should he think I know where the arms are, when Ferris doesn't? Why?"

Stephen straightened. "Because you live here? Because you have always lived here? Think. Is there anywhere in Ardinford that would make a suitable —and safe — hiding place for those machine guns?"

Alison moved across to the door, her brow ridged in thought. "No ... No ... Not that I can think of. The Court is the largest place around here, and that has vast cellars, but ... No. Ellery would never store the armaments there. It would be too risky for him. Besides, surely, that would be the first place Ferris would look if he decided on a double-cross; he wouldn't need me to tell him that." She raised her head. "And we have no proof that he intends any such treachery, only Ellery's jumpy suspicions."

"If Ferris can't recover the diamonds, I should think Ellery Sugden might prove only too correct," said Stephen dryly. "Possession would mean everything, then."

Alison leaned her hot forehead against the wood of the door, staring out through the crack by the hinge at Whooms, who was lighting a cigarette. Her eyes travelled past him, in their limited range, to the store of drums and tools and gravel in the series of shallow arches that had been cut from the quarry face. The chalk was blindingly white, although in one section, by the nearest arch, heavily festooned with a wild rose bush whose delicate pink cups were wide-eyed in the fierce sunshine. To one side of this lay a pile of tree branches, ash saplings from the quarry itself, that had been cut down less than a month ago to provide wood for the camp-fires of the Brownies, who had always played their games and sung their songs there on summer camping expeditions – until Ellery Sugden had stepped in this year and re-shuffled the programme.

Suddenly, Alison stiffened, voices and images flashing across memory.

But, of course, that was it! No wonder Ellery was so afraid that she would remember: of all people, she was the one who had been given the greatest opportunity for recall.

She spun, excitedly. "Stephen! I think I can guess where the guns are; in fact, I'm sure." She laughed. "They're here. They've been here all the time."

Stephen stared at her. "Here?"

"Yes. In the quarry. Don't you remember? The army commandeered the place during the war. They had some kind of store or ammunition dump here. But not exposed like this, that would have been madness. They excavated deep tunnels in the chalk, down into the bed-rock. Those are the entrances, over there, those arches cut into the chalk face. After the army moved out, the tunnels were still there, for years barricaded with heavy wooden shutters. But you know what children are like! Gradually, the planking was smashed, and the more adventurous among the village youngsters used to play down there, until one summer a boy broke his leg, and was trapped in one of the tunnels and not found for twenty-four hours. I was very small, but I can recall the panic. And, after that, the tunnels were bricked up. But they wouldn't have been filled in, that would have been too difficult and too costly, so they must still be there, behind those arches."

Stephen came and stood beside her. He applied his eye to the chink of light.

"Yes," he said slowly. "That sounds a perfect place for a cache. Probably one of those brick backings is false, or Ellery Sugden might even have done the whole thing properly and removed the brickwork, to re-brick it again after the guns were in position. That wouldn't have been hard, I imagine."

"And the wall would be knocked down again when he was ready to move them out?"

"Yes. The effort would be worthwhile because he'd be

sure the stuff was safe. He could hide it inside, then a quick coat of whitewash, a rub with chalk, and hey presto! Construction machinery could have been used to bring the goods in, before Ferris and his team arrived – after all, to the unversed eye, one earth-mover or dirt-lorry looks very like the next, and vehicles seem to have been trundling the lanes for weeks."

"And nobody's given those tunnels a thought for nigh on twenty years. The quarry belongs to Sugden Court, and no one comes here." Alison looked at Stephen and smiled without humour. "Ellery must have received an awful shock when he remembered my once-yearly cavortings down here. Well, it wasn't too difficult to re-site the Brownies and their camp – just offer them something too good to refuse – but he must have suddenly realized, when he saw me with Ferris, that I might let drop a hint about the army and their tunnelling. He'd believe that just being in the quarry would bring it to my mind. And, for all that Ellery was only the warehouseman, if anything happened to those guns he'd be in dire trouble with the dealer, wouldn't you say? So he wasn't very safe with me sitting here – especially if he didn't trust Ferris. If Ferris started probing and asking questions about the area –" Alison glanced sideways at Stephen, the corners of her mouth twitching: "Ferris is not stupid: he would have understood what a marvellous place it would make for storage, as well as for the transaction. And he'd have guessed the truth – that the goods were there, beneath his nose, without him having been aware of the fact. All he had to do was provide the cash – the diamonds – then he would have been told to load up, and away. Yes, very clever … And if the guns are already here, even without the payment –" She laughed aloud. "So, for the first time, Stephen, we possess a trump card."

"How do you mean?"

"We can barter with Ferris for our release. He needs the guns, and we want our freedom. Simple."

"Alison—"

She stared at him. "We can work something out, I'm sure we can. Stephen, he's not a monster, I'm sure he'd let us go."

"He wouldn't be able to, Alison: every policeman in the country would be on his tail."

"We could give him our word—"

"Alison! Those are guns you are talking about handing over to him, not jelly beans. Guns! They kill people. Alison, Ferris is a killer. And, if he once guessed you knew where the stuff was, how long do you think you could hold out against him? There'd be no barter. What you've had to suffer up till now would seem as nothing, his sport, that's all. If he wanted information from you, Alison, he'd get it, believe me. And it wouldn't be freedom we tasted in return. If you tell him where the guns are, you sign our death warrants."

She looked at him rebelliously. "He doesn't want to harm us, Stephen, I know he doesn't. He wouldn't allow Ellery to kill us—"

"It suits him, Alison, at the moment. Don't you see? Oh, I'm sure he finds you very fascinating," Stephen said bitterly, "but not *that* fascinating, my love. He's not going to jeopardize the success of this whole operation for a girl's pretty face."

Alison clasped her hands. "Stephen, if we go with Ellery in his Land-Rover, there's no guarantee he is going to let us go, either. In fact, quite the reverse, I should say. If we are a threat to Ferris, then we are an even greater one to Ellery Sugden. It would be a case of out of the frying-pan into the fire. He might kill us both, quite easily."

"Not easily," said Stephen tersely. "There's only one of him, and crippled at that. I'll take a gamble with him, rather than with Ferris and company. Out of this pit we may stand a chance."

"Then your vote is to trust Ellery? To go?"

"To go, anyway – if we have the opportunity. We'll think of something else, later."

"Stephen –?" She broke off, not looking at him.

"Yes?"

"What will happen to them? If we escape from here, and go to the police – what will happen to them? To Ferris and his men?"

"A nice strong jail for thirty years, or so, I hope."

She said nothing else, but crossed to the chink by the door again, and stood peering out. Her arms were hugged tightly around her body as if she were, suddenly, very cold.

"Is Whooms still on his tar-drum?" Stephen asked from behind her. She nodded, and he hoisted her to the window for a better view. At that instant she saw Ellery Sugden come out of the first hut and call across to the fat man, and wave a beckoning arm.

Whooms picked up his rifle, spun his cigarette butt into the water below him, and ambled down the ramp. Alison watched him cross in front of their prison-hut and walk slowly towards Sugden. Then both men disappeared inside the cliff-shadowed hut where Ferris had gone much earlier.

"By Christ, he's done it, then," said Stephen, when she relayed the news. "He's really done it. He's got rid of Whooms." He put his hand on the door.

"Ellery said to wait for ten minutes," warned Alison. "He has to remove the bar yet, and then make sure that Whooms and Ferris are safely occupied, before we make a move to the Land Rover."

"Oh, then we'll do what Ellery said," grinned Stephen jauntily. "There's just time to take out this other board." He knelt on the floor.

Alison crouched beside him. "It doesn't matter, now," she said, folding her hand over his.

"No. But there's a certain satisfaction in showing Ferris that we'd have gone, anyway." He tore at the planking, only to pause a few minutes later and say in a hushed, listening voice: "Somebody's coming."

There was a faint sound from the door behind them, the creak of wood … and soft footsteps, receding. Then, in the distance, Ferris's voice raised in a shout.

The seconds passed. There was no further sound, no voices, only their own breathing, and, once, the far off report of a shot from the direction of the south wood; Richlyn Taggard was evidently still filling the larder. Still they waited. Soft footsteps, and a little shush-shushing sound which they could not identify, then again, silence.

Stephen went to the crack by the door, but could see nobody. Whooms was still absent and, when he lifted Alison to check through the window, so were the other two men. The quarry floor was deserted.

"Shall we give it a try?" asked Stephen quietly.

She nodded.

Very gently, he turned the door handle. It gave beneath his fingers, and the door swung open. No lock, no bar, and no one to be seen. And they knew that the guard at the top of the main track was unable to scan their section of the quarry, for bushes and a curve of the cliff obscured his view.

For one glorious, golden moment, despite all urgency, Stephen halted and held his face to the sun and took his first deep breath of fresh air since he had been incarcerated in the hut. Just to breathe in the sunlight was a joy. Alison clasped his hand.

When they finally reached the rock-fall, there was no sign of Ellery Sugden beside the Land-Rover.

"Up you go," said Stephen, boosting Alison into the rear of the vehicle and swinging himself up beside her. He thrust aside the paraphernalia around him to give himself room to manoeuvre, and peered forward. "No keys."

"Do you think it's a trap?" Alison was still uneasy, prickles of fear running up and down her spine.

"Well, we'll soon find out," said Stephen, philo-sophically, scrambling under the rug and tugging her down beside him. He covered her head, took her into his arms. And the endless minutes limped by.

"Something's wrong," whispered Alison. "I don't know why, but I feel it. Ellery should be here by now." Her head came up.

"Lie down," said Stephen. "Give him a moment or two, you don't know what's holding him up."

Alison remained where she was, staring at the long grass at the foot of the ramp. Above that were the bushes and then the rearing quarry walls. And, beyond it all, lay Ardinford and home and the sun-drenched, flower-studded fields of freedom.

Her gaze ranged downwards again, through shadowy leaves, and petals falling. The flicker of butterflies. A dance of water. And everything still. All-pervading was the hot and dusty schoolroom smell of chalk. She turned her head to the rock-fall and the long grass beside her. Silence. Waving daisy heads. And flies buzzing.

And then she froze. An arm was crawling through the swaying grasses. No, not crawling, that was an illusion of the breeze and light, but lying there, flung outwards, inert, the hand like a white starfish spread, with the wrist ending in a well-remembered blue plaid shirt.

"Stephen," she croaked. She tugged at his shoulder and he turned in surprise, trying to grasp her as she slipped away from him over the tail of the Land-Rover. He stretched forward.

"Alison. What the —"

And then he, too, saw what had attracted her attention, and swung out of the vehicle to crouch beside her.

It was Ellery all right, lying face upwards in the blowing grass beside them, his legs half in, half out, of a patch of nettles. There was a small black hole just behind his ear.

Alison groped forward. She had no need to take the limp hand in hers to know that he was dead. But he was still warm, still pliant, not yet stiffened into the hideous rigor of death, his eyes open, staring at the sky.

The sun burned down the chalk cliff, searing their

eyeballs. A brown leaf expanded into the wings of a tortoiseshell butterfly and fluttered off above their heads.

Alison went on feeling for the pulse in the outstretched wrist until Stephen eased her gently backwards against him, to hold her in the crook of his arm.

"He's dead," he said. "Ellery's dead."

"Oh, yes, he's very dead," said Ferris's familiar voice behind them, itself as harsh and cold as death. And his black shadow slithered over them and blotted out the sun.

Thirteen

Alison turned her head slowly. Ferris was standing barely an arm's length away from them, against the sunlight, and behind him, one at each elbow, hovered the figures of Whooms and Dillman. At Ferris's signal, his men moved forward in one easy stride and hauled Stephen roughly to his feet.

"Tie him up," said Ferris. "Lock him in the hut. Securely, this time. I'll take Sugden's body to the diggings and get rid of him there. It'll be safer. Curly should be with the machinery, somewhere, making noises like a road gang. When we've disposed of Sugden we'll both give the Court the once over, and see if the guns have been hidden there all this time. It's worth a try. We're just about stumped with the diamonds: we've been over that churchyard like a fine-toothed comb. If the dealer won't deal ..." He broke off and kicked at Sugden's body with his toe. The dark eyes were like stone. "No one tries to double-cross me," he said, in a deadly voice.

Hurriedly, Alison scrambled upright, and made to follow Stephen to the hut, but Ferris's hand shot out and grabbed her wrist.

"Not you, Goldilocks, I'm putting you in the main building, for the time being; we'll keep you and Brand separated and perhaps out of mischief. And when I return I'd like a word with you both – to find out just why Sugden was so anxious to whisk you away from me. Dead or alive, it didn't seem to matter much, did it? What fascinating piece of information do you hold that he didn't want me to possess?"

She stood, imprisoned by his hand, staring at him with frightened eyes.

Ferris waited until his two men had finished locking Stephen in the small hut, then shouted over his shoulder: "Dillman! Whooms! Hoist Sugden's body into the back of his Land-Rover and cover it with the rug there. The sooner I get going, the better. Then, Dillman, you may have the pleasure of keeping an eye on the girl –" He felt Alison stiffen under his hand and smiled down at her without warmth. "Yes. That should make you think twice, shouldn't it? ... And Whooms, you take yourself back to your tar-drum and keep watch till I come back."

"Boss," protested Whooms, "Hoat and I were just going to change duties – that's what Dillman came down to tell me – Hoat's having a fine old time up there, doing nothing in the shade of a tree. The glare in this quarry hurts my eyes, and I've been here for hours –"

"I don't give a damn how many hours you've been here," said Ferris. "You'll do as I say. You can all play musical chairs later."

"I thought –"

"Your thoughts will keep for the long dark evenings," snapped Ferris. "Now get up there on that ramp, and keep awake. If I didn't have such a bloody useless crew we wouldn't be in this mess."

"And I'm to watch the girl?" Dillman laughed under his breath.

Ferris scowled at him. "Watch her, not touch her ... We all know your disgusting habits." He tugged on Alison's arm, towing her across the uneven surface of the quarry floor. "And you, my lady, will sit and grow good, do you understand? No stupid attempts to escape – you can't possibly succeed – and even if you did, well" – he grinned – "I'd surely shoot Brand, so don't forget it."

He flung her into the first hut with such force that she

lost her balance and landed on the floor. But he turned without a backward glance and kicked the door shut behind him.

Alison picked herself up from the dirty boards, rubbing her bruised elbow, in time to hear Ferris shout to his men: "If either of them try anything while I'm gone, shoot them!"

Outside, an engine roared to life. The Land-Rover ground through its gears, and she heard the vehicle snarling up the main track through the quarry. She stood stock still, listening to the receding truck with a sickeningly thudding heart. Ferris had gone. She pushed back her hair with an unsteady hand. Ferris had gone, leaving her here alone with Dillman.

Dillman, quite frankly, terrified her. He had a way of looking at her that stripped her naked. True, apart from that first, terrible experience with him in the hut – she swallowed, feeling the sickness within her, and poured herself a mug of water with shaking hands, for that was something to be relegated to the realms of nightmare – he had not touched her. Or, at least, had not touched her in any way that could not have been construed as purely accidental. But she had heard the other men talking, laughing about his prowess and his deviations. There had been a girl – no, two girls – and both now dead, after Dillman's ministrations. She took another gulp of water. Besides, it was not just the talk, there was the way her scalp crawled when he came near her, and again, in nightmare, she felt his long fingers on her shrinking flesh and caught the scent of him, not sweat, or chalk dust, but a strong animal smell that made her heave.

Still, Ferris would be back soon, Ferris stood between her and Dillman. She had only to sit here, quietly, and wait. She would not venture outside the hut, she need not even open the door.

But the door was opened for her. It swung back with a crash and a rush of sunlight. And Dillman stood there in the entrance grinning like a wolf's head at her.

He said nothing, just lounged against the doorpost and went on grinning, his teeth white in his sharp-featured face. His profile was cruel, but perhaps more weasel than wolf, she thought, feeling the hot surge of blood in her head, and the thump of her frightened heart. Yes, that was it; he reminded her of a weasel, cunning and wily and cruel. But he would never dare to touch her, never dare to harm her: Ferris would be back. There was nothing Dillman could do to her. Nothing.

"What do you want?" she asked coldly.

"I thought you might be lonely."

"Not for your company."

"Ferris will be a long time gone: Ferris has to take care of your other friend."

She rounded on him. "There was no need to kill Ellery Sugden."

"Oh, the boss didn't do it entirely on your account, don't flatter yourself. He knew Sugden was going to inform the dealer about our difficulties, and take away any chance Ferris had of stalling for a few more days. Then, when he saw Sugden remove that bar on your hut, well , that was the final nail in his coffin –" Dillman shrugged. "But we waited to see what he'd arranged for you to do."

"You hold life very cheaply."

"Of course. That's the nature of our business ... Although we're usually sure of a little fun first." He looked her over with his bright eyes.

Alison hung on to her self control.

"I think you'd better go outside and attend to whatever you are supposed to be doing."

He said softly: "Oh, there's plenty of time for that." And he came forward, smiling, his teeth gleaming very whitely between his lips.

"Don't you dare touch me," she said, taking a swift step away from him. Her back came up against the shelf.

"I always like a challenge. How do you intend to stop

me?" He stretched out a lazy arm and hooked it over her shoulder.

Alison shook him off and ducked sideways.

"If you touch me, you'll have to answer to Ferris –"

Dillman's gaze was bright and sardonic. "Oh, I always answer to Ferris."

He cornered her again and dragged her, struggling, across to the bed. And, as she opened her lips to scream, he closed his hand hard over her mouth.

"Don't do it, sweetie," he warned. "You can scream as much as you like, but no one is going to help you. Hoat would never leave his post at the top of the quarry, and Whooms cares nothing about your welfare, he still carries your scars ... However, I dislike the noise, and each time you scream I shall have to hit you. Do you follow?" He flung her forward, sprawling, on to the bed, and then he was on top of her, pinning her down with the weight of his body.

Alison squirmed wildly beneath him, scratching, kicking, but fighting a losing battle as he clawed at her clothing.

"Stop it," he panted. "Stop it! Lie still, before I knock you still, you little hell-cat ... What possible difference can this make to you?" He gave an ugly little laugh. "Me or Ferris, where's the bloody difference, sweetie?"

She twisted her head sideways, gasping up at him: "Ferris will kill you ... When he returns, he'll surely kill you for this."

Dillman's hand caught her hair, yanking her head backwards and twisting it so that she was forced to look up into his face. There was a red glare at the back of his eyes.

"Ferris ... will ... do ... nothing!" he said. He pulled at her hair again. "When I've finished with you, pussy-cat, you'll be dead: you'll be shot while trying to escape." He smiled his thin, cruel smile. "Ferris is a realist: he may not entirely believe me, but he'll face the fact that one live member of this party is worth more than one dead girl. And he needs me." He forced his mouth down on hers.

Alison's free hand came out and grabbed at his left ear, but he struck her away and went on to press her knees up and out beneath him. His arms and legs were like steel wire with a strength that was deceptive in their slenderness. There was no way she was going to be free of him. He had her, and he knew it.

Suddenly she stilled and went limp underneath him, fighting against him no longer. For a few seconds Dillman waited, covering her, thinking she might be playing possum, but when she continued to lie quiescent on the bed, he eased his body on hers so that her head was no longer locked under him, and she found that she was able to move her other arm. For a moment it lay numb beside him on the rumpled blanket, then, blindly, her fingers crept over his taut body in a soft caressing motion before moving over her own bare leg and sliding gently across her thigh, down over her knee, down, fluttering again for a brief spell against his groping arm, and on until her questing hand reached her sandal. Gently, desperately, she withdrew the six-inch nail she had hidden there earlier that morning. When she had accomplished that task, she released her breath on a small sigh and raised her arms slowly above her head in a strangely abandoned gesture. She no longer fought him. She lay defenceless, ready to allow him to do as he wished. And, believing her to be tamed, Dillman relaxed his guard to avail himself of this swift surrender.

As his face hovered above her, Alison brought both her hands together on the long nail and, tensing like a coiled spring, struck out with all the frantic power she could bring to bear, straight at one of those glittering, glass-green eyes.

Dillman uttered a short, high-pitched, half-animal scream, and collapsed over her in a gush of blood and water. His hand clawed up wildly once, then that, too, was still, and there was a soft smack as it fell limply against the wall. He lay there leaden on her, quite motionless, like an iron bar that she could not lift, and she whimpered beneath his weight, feeling the awful retching starting in her stomach. She was going to be sick, and there was nothing she could do about it.

Again and again, she repeated to herself, in desperate little whimpers: "Oh God – Oh God – Oh God."

She pushed feebly at the heavy, inert body with her hands. Her strength had gone, and so, too, had her courage. Only one bright spark of will enduring in her brain prevented her from losing the precarious hold she now had on reason, and keeling over entirely into hysteria, or some black and bottomless pit. Certainly, when Ferris heaved Dillman's corpse from her, heaven knew how many minutes later, she was still conscious and coherent.

Ferris wasted no time in asking what had happened: the whole affair was all to obvious. He knew Dillman and, a little, he knew Alison. He pulled her to her feet and watched her totter to the door, then he wrapped the crumpled sheet around Dillman's body before taking her a mug of water.

"Here, drink this." His voice was smooth, his eyes expressionless. He said: "Where did you find the nail?" But, no, that was not what he meant, there were dozens of nails scattered around outside that she could have picked up at any time and carried about with her. In her blouse? In her shoe? The question was, why? To defend herself, as she had done today? Or was the answer more premeditated than that? "I suppose I was to be the lucky one?" She looked at him mutely. "Was I?" He shook her, spilling the water. "Did you intend to use that nail on me? To stick me like a pig?"

"No," she said faintly, and tried to wrench free but he held her facing him.

"No? And am I supposed to believe that?" He shook her again, harder this time, and enough to make her teeth rattle.

She gave a little cry, more of protest than of pain, and said, very clearly: "It was not for you. It was –" But, then, she could not tell him what the nail had been for, and thus reveal Stephen's work on the floorboards.

"You're lying to me, aren't you?"

"No," she repeated. "It was not for you." If he did not believe her she no longer cared. That it had not been for him seemed, if anything, the greater betrayal of Stephen.

The colour was coming back into her face, and her voice was growing stronger, though a trace of desperation remained in her eyes. What colour were her eyes? wondered Ferris. He was never quite able to make up his mind. Blue? Grey? They were as changeable as water, although now as dull as lead. And, because he wanted to believe her, he told himself that her voice held the ring of truth. Besides, he knew Dillman ... A useful man gone, sure, but reprisals against the girl would not bring him back.

Ferris said: "Get cleaned up. Take off those things. There's a clean shirt on a hook over there, use that." Ironical that the garment should belong to Dillman. He pushed her inside the hut, eased the Land-Rover closer to the building, and called across to the man he had brought back to the quarry with him. "Curly, fetch Brand, will you? And tell Whooms to come and help me here." Then he followed Alison inside. He slipped a bottle of whisky from his pocket and stood it on the table.

"What – What are you going to do?" She looked at him in apprehension.

"With you?" A smile touched his thin mouth, and was gone. His eyes took in the brief garment she was now wearing; the long, bare, lovely legs. "Nothing very dreadful, if you answer a few questions. I want to know what secrets you had with Sugden. Your boyfriend will be my guarantee of your good faith, that is all."

"You mean you are going to hurt him?"

He looked at her measuringly, wondering how much more pressure she could take, but knowing he was not in this game to be gentle. Now was the time to force her, to ask his questions while she was still shaken. A little work upon Brand –

"Not if you please me." He moved and stood staring out of the dirty window. There were moments when the whole world seemed to him equally dirty.

When Whooms arrived he helped Ferris to stow the dead man's body in the back of the Land-Rover until it could be taken up to the excavations. And Stephen was brought into the hut some two minutes later. His ankles had been untied so that he could walk, but his wrists were still bound firmly behind him. Ferris ordered him to be fastened to a chair.

"A slight precaution," he said, smiling thinly.

A few loops of cord from Curly, and Stephen was trussed and immobile before them.

"Now," said Ferris, "I want –"

What Ferris wanted was destined to remain undisclosed because, at that instant, the door opened on a breath of hot, chalk-laden air, and there on the threshold, framed in sunlight, stood the Reverend Kelvin Hunter.

He came quietly into the room, and closed the door behind him. For frozen seconds no one spoke.

Then Alison said faintly: "Father –"

Kelvin Hunter might have appeared like an apparition before them, standing graceful and immaculate, with one shoulder against the door, but the small, deadly, automatic pistol he was holding in his hand was certainly no mirage.

Alison made to move across the room towards him, but Hunter said sharply: "Stay where you are, Alison." His glance ranged over the other occupants of the hut, then flicked from Ferris to Alison, and back again.

"What," he said, "is she doing here?"

This time Alison did move; she moved and spoke.

"Thank God, Father," she said. "Oh, thank God, you've come," and she was across the room in three steps to stand at his side.

Ferris said: "I had no choice; she and Brand were snooping around. I had to keep them here." He shook off the paralysis that appeared to have him in its grip and went on levelly: "I presume you have come to deal?"

Hunter turned his pale eyes on him. "That is correct."
He swung back to his daughter. "Are you all right,
Alison?"

She nodded. "But Stephen—"

But Stephen had cottoned on to the situation more
quickly than she had. He said wearily: "Leave it, Alison,
leave it—" She stared across at him in surprise, and he went
on: "Not the cavalry, love. Meet the Reverend Kelvin
Hunter—the dealer."

"The dealer?" Alison's voice went in on a rasp. "My
father's come to deal with Ferris?"

Hunter continued speaking to Ferris, and gave a little
twist of smile. "And not before time, it would seem. Soon
the whole damned world will know why you and your men
are here." He turned and glanced at Alison, then back at
Ferris, and his voice was like the winter wind. "I hope, for
all your sakes, that no harm has come to my daughter."

Ferris avoided Alison's eyes. His nostrils looked pinched,
his face white, but she realized this was not the outward
sign of apprehension, or fear, but of anger. Ferris was
savagely angry. He kept his voice steady with difficulty.
"You have come to finalize arrangements?"

Hunter gave a faint smile. "You can meet my terms? I
imagined you might be in difficulties."

"I need a few more days in which to marshal payment,
that is all. There has been a slight hitch in our financial
plans."

"Indeed? You were to pay in uncut diamonds, were you
not? A suitable arrangement all round. Untraceable,
portable, and easily saleable. But not, at the moment—
available—would you say?" Hunter's voice was deadly.

Ferris said: "Sugden told you?"

Hunter glanced at him in surprise. "No. I did not confer
with Sugden. It would not have been—tenable. Or wise. To
him, I was a shadow with a purse-string; someone to plan
and to finance and to tell him what to do. However, enough
of that ... Let it suffice that I am still prepared to deal with

you, Ferris; to wait, even, if I have the truth." He twitched his gun. "I am not an unreasonable man. With my connections I might even be able to help you solve your problems – for a price. Lost, stolen, or strayed, Ferris? And where?"

Alison glanced sideways and saw Ferris's face like stone.

Hunter went on: "Ah, I see you fear repercussions. But my daughter I can handle, and she will travel with me, if it should become necessary – Mr and Mrs Upright on a flight to South America. Brand, you may dispose of as you think fit – I imagine in that department your ingenuity will prove greater than mine."

Ferris said, in a curiously flat voice: "The missing diamonds – if it was not Sugden who informed you, then who?"

"Come, come, Ferris. We are not all the ignorant turnip-tops that you seem to think, and you have been cutting a wide swathe of disruption through Ardinford, in one way and another ... It was our contact who – alas, with us no longer – unwittingly provided me with the suspicion that your payment might prove to be no longer in your safe keeping. You have been drawing attention to your incompetence." His voice took on a sarcastic note. "It was exceedingly careless of you, Ferris, to allow a child to make a clay model incorporating two of your uncut stones."

Alison said faintly: "Dix's horse with the diamond eyes. How did you find out about that?"

Her father looked down at her and raised an eyebrow. "Hardly a horse, my dear, even to my untutored gaze. A cat. A clay cat with diamond eyes."

"Miss Chubb!" She stared at him in disbelief. "Miss Chubb was your go-between?"

"And who more suitable, my dear? Within a radius of ten miles, or so, she went everywhere, met everyone – her and her damned religious tracts. It would have been exceedingly difficult for anybody to pin-point one particular contact. Even Sugden had convinced himself that she was operating via one of those large houses just outside Redeham. He followed her once ..." Hunter's tone was edged. "Anyhow, everyone was used to her peculiar ways and, equally, no one ever paid the slightest heed to anything she said. I was quite safe, even if she had inadvertently blurted out something of my business, nobody would have believed her. Besides, although she knew rather more than was good for her, she was, after all, involved in little except carrying messages and being my eyes and ears. It was unfortunate that she saw Ferris's men with the Taggard child, up on the Leap, because she was able to connect them with his death, and then with Sugden and myself and our – transaction. And that was dangerous. However, I was able to persuade her to keep quiet." He half smiled and added: "She would do anything I asked, you must have been aware of that: I was her saviour, her benefactor, her · guardian angel. Without me she was finished –"

"The destroying angel," said Stephen quietly from his corner.

For the first time since he had entered the room, Kelvin Hunter rested his pale gaze on the bound man for more than a couple of seconds. His eyes were the colour of ice, and as cold.

"Ah, Brand." The voice was silk, but that, too, chilled Stephen's blood. "So you are still with us? And still being a nuisance, I see. Well, that is one little problem I can irradicate here and now." He raised his automatic pistol and, quite clearly in the stillness, there came the tiny click of metal as he cocked the weapon. Stephen's face went rigid with horror as he stared straight into that black and deadly steel eye, but there was no way he could avoid what he knew must follow: he was the proverbial sitting duck; sitting, trussed, and expertly centred.

For an immobile second, Alison stared at her father, then suddenly comprehending what he was about to do, lunged forward. But she was too late. Even as she caught his hand, a pistol shot reverberated round the room.

There was the hiss of a sharp, indrawn breath, and the Reverend Hunter jerked and seemed to slacken in the middle. He collapsed against Alison, then fell away from her, catching his arm over the table's edge and hanging there motionless for a second before slithering slowly to the floor.

Fourteen

Ferris gently lowered the gun in his hand. For maybe ten seconds, maybe longer, nobody moved, nobody spoke. Alison was aware of Stephen staring across the room, chalk-faced, but still very much alive, his eyes riveted on her father who now lay in a crumpled heap upon the floor.

Curly was the first to find his tongue. As the echoes of the shot rocked into silence, he rounded on Ferris.

"What the bloody hell did you do that for? You've certainly screwed up things for us this time. How do you expect to get the armaments without him? We're finished ..."

Ferris stood with his face like a mask. "And do you think we wouldn't have been finished with him alive? Be your age, Curly. Can you imagine how he'd have reacted once the girl told him what we'd done to her? She's his daughter: we've not exactly been treating her with kid gloves." He gestured with his gun. "No. A bullet was our only chance. Remember, she *is* his daughter, and we still hold her, and she is going to provide us with everything we want."

He turned to Alison, who had dropped, dry-eyed, to her knees beside her father. Ferris yanked her to her feet, and she saw the mask crumble and a devil look out of his eyes. "Oh, yes, you bitch, you played me for a sucker, right enough, didn't you? For sheer duplicity, you sure beat them all. But nobody does that to me – and lives." He struck her twice across the face, savagely, first with his left hand and then with his right. As she reeled he jerked her upright and pulled her against him, twisting her hair around her throat. He felt he would like to strangle her, to take that rope of shining hair and pull it tight, tight, until she could no longer breathe ... He found his hands were shaking.

Stephen shouted, straining at his bonds: "Leave her alone."

Whirling, Curly rammed a dirty handkerchief into Stephen's mouth before demanding: "Do you think she knows where the stuff is, Ferris?"

"He was the rector," said Ferris, relaxing his hold on Alison's throat. "The guns are probably hidden somewhere in his church; the crypt, perhaps."

"That church doesn't possess a crypt," protested Curly, "and there are no crates or boxes anywhere around the place, we searched thoroughly when we were looking for the diamonds."

"Well, we'll have another look – with her, this time. We can search the rectory, too –" He paused. "If we wait until dusk, I'll put on Hunter's priestly dog-collar and dark jacket and pass for a visiting clergyman. I shall say I'm being shown round by the rector's daughter, if anyone comes poking about. She can think up some plausible story: she's very good at that kind of thing, with her big innocent eyes –" He swung on Alison with a flash of naked ferocity. "God all bloody mighty, but I could kill you! Here and now, without a qualm, but I need you, for the moment. After that –" He smiled at her, and again a devil looked out of his eyes. "After that, I will make you sorry that you were ever born. I will –" he let fly a stream of invective that would have lent colour to a dockyard. In the wooden hut, most of the obscenities went over Alison's head. She blinked in a dazed kind of fashion, her brain still numb with grief, and shook her head from side to side.

"I knew nothing about all this," she whispered. "Nothing. I had no idea my father was the one you called the dealer. No idea at all –"

"Spare me the 'innocent abroad' approach," said Ferris

viciously. "You will get me into the church, or the rectory, or wherever your father has so cunningly hidden those machine guns – and then you will pay. Believe me, you will pay. I will see you crawl in the gutter ... You may dwell a little upon what that might mean while I am planning our departure."

Alison said quietly: "There are no guns in the church or rectory. They are –"

"I remember, now," broke in Curly, excitedly. "A lot of hampers and cartons were carried into the rectory last week-end – on Saturday evening and Sunday morning. I helped with a few of them myself, while you and the boys were trying to locate the missing stones. You know I arrived in Ardinford a few days before you and the rest of the lads, to supervise the delivery of some machinery, and to set up things here, well, Sugden asked me if I'd mind giving him a hand as he was ferrying to and fro with his truck. He knew me a little by then. Anyhow, the boxes and baskets were supposed to have come from the village pageant – you saw the show yourself, on Saturday afternoon, when you were searching for the Taggard kid – and I was told they contained stuff to be stored in the rector's attics."

"Which is exactly what it was," said Alison dully. "The guns –"

"Shut up," said Ferris. "You've laughed up your sleeve at us for the last time, my fancy lady ... Curly, Whooms, lock them both in the other hut until I'm ready to take the girl back to the village. And then put Hunter's body in the truck along with Dillman's; we'll get rid of them later." He stretched out his hand to the bottle. "God, but I could do with a drink."

Alison watched the men cut Stephen free and support him to the door. Then she said very softly to Ferris: "What makes you think I'll help you, in any way at all? If Stephen and I are, in effect, already dead –" She glanced down, still dry-eyed, at her father.

Ferris gave a bitter smile. "Oh, you will help me, make

very sure of that. There are many ways to die; some easy, some agonizingly hard. You cannot begin to conceive the evils that might lie in store. I can give Brand the easy way out – a quick bullet when I am through, or you can have him, piece by piece, for as long as you stand out against me. Piece by piece! Do you doubt that? And when you hold the last shred of his flesh, then I will start on you ... And remember one small point: with or without you, I shall still have my way. With your co-operation, my path will be a little smoother, that is all." His voice dropped grimly. "As will the path of anyone I chance to meet."

His hands came down to grip her shoulders. Even through his hate, his body played traitor and wanted her. Well, he told himself, he would have her, and brutally: he was finished with finesse. Perhaps Dillman had had the right idea about women, after all – take them, and break them ...

They faced each other in silence for a few seconds longer, until Whooms came back and grasped Alison's arm, and Ferris watched them walk away from him, through the open door into the sunlight, and across the bone-white quarry floor. A small breeze lipped the chalk-dust under their feet, stirring it like ashes.

When Alison had been deposited, none too gently, in the small prison-hut along with Stephen, a disgruntled Whooms took up his usual place on the ramp, while Curly departed to assist Ferris with whatever plans were being made for that evening.

The instant the door had closed behind her and the key had scraped its way into the lock, Stephen was down on his knees, uncovering the hole he had made in the floor.

"Come on," he said. "Two more nails to prise from this loose board, and then there should be enough space for us to squeeze through and crawl under the hut. We shall have to go now, as soon as we can, we can't afford to wait for darkness in case Ferris decides to separate us before then. And we have no idea how long he and Curly will remain safely in the other building. For a nice long session, I hope: I noticed Ferris had brought a bottle." He glanced up at Alison, aware that she was unusually silent, and was relieved to see that she was not in tears. Not for the first time, he thanked his lucky stars for providing him with a non-hysterical partner: at this moment, he could not have coped with a wailing woman. She had had more than her share of hell in the past couple of days, but it was essential that she did not crack now. He flashed her another glance: she did not look in a state of imminent collapse. Her face resembled wood.

After a few more seconds work on the nail under his hands, Stephen said: "I'm sorry about your father, Alison – sorry he's dead, I mean."

Her eyes lifted and met his. She said slowly: "Do you believe I knew about my father and this arms deal?"

Stephen laughed. "Of course not. I know you, Alison, my sweet. And you're not devious, or crooked, or cruel. You'd never have been a party to anything like that. If there is one thing in this whole crazy world I would stake my life on, it is that. Your straightforwardness and honesty."

She smiled at him. "Thank you, anyway, for that."

"Did you imagine I wouldn't believe you?"

"Not really. But I'm beginning to lose my grip on reality a little, I think ... Stephen! How could my father have done such a thing? How could he have mixed himself up with a deal like this, trading in illegal or stolen arms?" She sounded bewildered. "And how could I not have known? I loved him, I thought he loved me –"

"Of course he loved you. Perhaps too much."

"Then why? Why?"

"Who knows? Power? Hate? Some kind of twisted conviction? A chance to score off life? Or perhaps he was determined not to lose you. Perhaps, at the back of his mind, he had decided to go out on an exploit like this, then off to South America – with you."

"But I would never have gone. Didn't he realize that?"

"No," said Stephen quietly, "I don't suppose he did. And, if it had come to the crunch, would you really have deserted him? Besides, who knows what other schemes he had in store? Certainly, I believe I was scheduled for the way out."

"Then he sorely underestimated me," said Alison, taking the nail extricated from the board, head first, from Stephen's fingers. "I am not my father's child for nothing." Her lips tightened grimly. "And there's a thought! Are you still willing to take me on?"

Stephen paused in his task for an instant and put his hand on hers. "Cross my heart —"

She said: "He was a good man, Stephen, he was! He did so much to help people, they relied on him —"

"I know. But human nature is full of contradictions. Something happens to upset the balance, and then — bang! Perhaps, with your father, the trigger was a little of a lot of things. Who can tell? He was a strong, secretive man."

"Yes," said Alison slowly. "And I think his faith was lost a long time ago, and he found nothing to replace it. Although even I didn't appreciate quite how much he had changed after my mother died. But the signs were there, simmering beneath the surface, if I hadn't closed my eyes to them. He became a kind of actor-manager, dressing-up, carrying out a part, manipulating his little people on his little stage — and then, it seems, he suddenly had the chance to manipulate on a larger scale — to be god-like — to destroy ..." She turned to Stephen. "Was that what you meant, back there, when you called him the destroying angel?"

Stephen wrestled with the recalcitrant remaining nail in the loosened floor-board, giving it a couple more twists before he answered her.

"That was what Miss Chubb called him, only I didn't understand, at the time, that she was referring to your father. When I eventually recalled her words I became side-tracked in quite a different direction —" His eyes flickered.

"But I remember, now, that it was on Sunday, just after morning service, outside the lychgate by the church, when Miss Chubb made her remark to me. Kelvin was standing beside the west door, still in his surplice. And it must have been him she meant. Only, I was too preoccupied to take much notice, and I was in a hurry, and ..."

"... No one ever paid any attention to Miss Chubb," said Alison sadly. "She cycled around and saw and heard far more than her scrambled brain could cope with. She must have known that my father was into something evil, but she was incapable of denouncing him. He had helped her, was always helping her, she couldn't manage without him, and she owed him too much to be the one to cause his downfall. She had to protect him. Keep silence. After Dix died, a direct result, she guessed, of meddling with these people and this affair, she didn't know what to do. She knew the rector was at the centre of these events. And, in the end, the knowledge killed her ... But she kept silent." Alison glanced at Stephen. "Except in that fleeting, involuntary remark to you."

"... Got it!" Stephen sat back on his heels, triumphant.

Alison threw him a puzzled look, then saw the nail he was holding between his fingers.

"You've finished?" she said. She peered into the dark hole. The smell of cool, sunless chalk came up to greet her. "We can get through?"

"We're going to have to," said Stephen tightly. "I'll go first. You know what to do. We've been over things often enough. I'll creep behind Whooms by way of the rock-fall, through the long grass and scrub there, which shouldn't prove too hazardous, and then, when I've successfully put him to sleep, you can help me tie him up ... I'll find a sizeable chunk of rock for a weapon on my travels ... Then you must continue along the ramp path as far as you can go without being seen from the first hut, that's about two-thirds of the way along, on the other side of the bushes." His eyes narrowed. "Meanwhile, I fire Whoom's gun at the petrol-tank of Ellery Sugden's Land-Rover, which is now parked by the bunker at the end of the first building, the truck explodes, traps the inmates of the hut and, hopefully, Hoat comes down from his position at the top of the quarry to see what is going on and assist in rescue operations – and we hot-foot it up the remainder of the ramp-path, on to the main track, behind Hoat. Does that sound all right to you?"

Alison looked dubious. "Are you sure a bullet will explode the petrol-tank? I know it always seems to do the trick on television, but –"

"Well, if it doesn't, I'm just going to have to keep popping away with the rifle, while you get clear."

"No!" said Alison. "No! I'm not going without you. I haven't been through all this, to lose you now. If you stay, I stay."

"You will do as I say."

"I will not!" Alison scowled at him furiously. "After everything we've been through, I'm not leaving without you."

"You have no choice."

She stared at him.

He said: "One of us must escape from here, tell the authorities what is going on, rescue those guns. You know that. If you are sensible and think about it, you know that."

"Why me?" she said obstinately. "Why does it have to be me?"

"Can you fire a rifle?"

"No, but –"

"I can." He failed to tell her that the only rifle he'd ever handled had been on a fun-fair range. "And keep your fingers crossed that the Land-Rover goes up in flames, then, with a bit of luck, the gas cylinders will explode: they're right beside the truck. We've got to keep Curly and Ferris out of action and induce Hoat to come down from his post, that's the only way either of us has any chance at all …"

"Will the explosion hurt them, the men in the hut?" asked Alison.

"I hope it hurts them very much indeed," said Stephen, with a glittering look. "I hope it bloody well kills them!" He took hold of her arm. "Now, come on. Follow me. And get ready to collect a few pieces of the cord that's lying around, for Whooms's bonds." He flicked his eyes over Alison's scanty attire and smiled slightly. "I'll use a piece of my shirt for a gag – you can't spare anything."

In less than sixty seconds, they had wriggled through the bolt-hole and come up at the back of the hut, against the quarry face, with little more than a few scrapes and scratches to show for their efforts. Stephen bent and picked up a jagged lump of chalk, hefting it in his hand.

"Stay here, Alison," he said. "Then when you see Whooms collapse, run like hell behind that scrub and over the rock-fall. Once we're in Whoom's position behind those hawthorns we should be safe enough. And, remember, this will be the only chance we have, if we muff it there'll be no second try."

But Alison knew that even better than he did. She hardly recognized this unshaven, hard-eyed, determined man as the gentle Stephen she had promised to marry such a short time ago. His face, under two days' growth of bristle, was mask-like and pale as wax. And he appeared quite ready to destroy.

With her heart hammering in her mouth, Alison watched Stephen's progress through the moving grasses. Whooms sat motionless on his drum, in the shade of the hawthorn tree, his rifle balanced beside him, his picture-paper drooping in his hand. His head drooped, too. He was, she thought, asleep.

The density of light seemed to shift a little behind the drowsing man, like a dance of shadows, and she saw Stephen rise and move quietly forward, holding the piece of rock steady in his hand. A curve of his arm upwards and a forcible swing down, and the rock crunched hard on the head of its unsuspecting victim. Whooms keeled over without a sound, pitching forward to the ground. As he fell, his outstretched arm caught the rifle-barrel, knocking the weapon from its standing perch and sweeping it over the edge of the ramp. Alison was halfway across the rock-fall before Whooms had completed his unconscious dive but, although she flung herself forward in a desperate flying tackle, she was too late to catch the toppling rifle. It fell with a loud, sickening splash into the oil-scummed water below them, and disappeared from view.

Alison stared at Stephen in horror. For a moment, neither of them spoke, then Stephen said, matter-of-factly: "Help me to prop him up." Together, they slid their arms under the fat man's flaccid shoulders and heaved him, inch by inch, back into a sitting position on the drum, with his spine against the small hawthorn tree. Stephen straightened the body, arranged the arms and legs neatly together, and began to tie them with pieces of cord. Whooms remained quite still, eyes closed.

"Have you killed him?" whispered Alison.

Stephen continued with his task, pulling at the knots callously. "I don't give a damn," he replied, in a low voice. He removed his shirt, ripped out a sleeve and made an efficient, and equally vicious job of gagging their one-time jailer. "There," he said quietly, when he had finished to his satisfaction, "let him get out of those in a hurry, if he can." He stepped back. "If anyone comes this way, he looks normal enough. They'll have to come right up on the ramp to find out otherwise." He fished in his pocket and pulled out the box of matches Alison had appropriated for him earlier.

"What are you going to do?" She eyed him fearfully.

He didn't answer her directly. "Get ready to run." He turned to race back down the ramp but she caught at his arm.

"Tell me what you intend to do. I'm not going anywhere, running or otherwise, unless I know what you're up to."

"The rifle's gone: we stand no chance without it."

"So?" She held on to him tightly.

"I'm going to drop a match in the Land-Rover's petrol-tank, that's all."

"That's all!" She glared at him. "You can't! You can't! You'll blow yourself sky-high and, even if you didn't, you'd never make it back up here before Hoat came gunning for you with his rifle – or Curly and Ferris came out at you with theirs. It's too far to run."

"I'm hoping," he said, "that the hut will go up along with the truck, that will scotch Curly and Ferris."

"You know it won't work. You know it won't! Not so that it will give you any chance at all. You know you'll be blown to pieces, one way or another. You'll never get clear. Can't you think of anything else?"

"I could always stand here and heave a few rocks," he said with bitter sarcasm.

That, she ignored. "Well, then. A little fire, perhaps. Just a little fire to bring Hoat down the track. Somewhere here, on the ramp ..." But no, that would leave Curly and Ferris free to commit whatever mayhem they chose. But there had to be some other way. She cast around her. There were rocks and sticks, but nothing more. She kicked at a slender branch of ash sapling which was jutting from the pile of branches once intended for camp-fires.

"Wait a minute," said Stephen slowly, staring down at the branches. "Perhaps there is another way, after all. It depends on how good my aim is. But I've had plenty of practice in recent weeks, thanks to the pageant –"

"What are you talking about?"

"A bow."

"A bow?"

"A longbow and arrows."

"A longbow and arrows!" Alison's voice rose on a despairing squeak. "Now I know you're crazy. Your sojourn in that hut must have turned your wits. What you are suggesting is just about as primitive as lobbing stones."

"I'm not talking about picking them off, one by one, as they come at me," said Stephen.

She stared at him dumbly, shaking her head.

He explained, patiently. "I mean fire-arrows. If I can get one into the back of the truck, start a blaze –" He measured the distance with his eyes. "It's not a difficult shot and, fortunately, the rear of the Land-Rover is towards me –" He looked at the vehicle measuringly again. "I'd better splash around a bit of petrol or something, I suppose – to speed up the blaze, and the bang. I think I saw a spare can of fuel in the back of the truck – Ellery usually carted one around for emergencies with the estate machinery – if not, there's plenty of diesel in those drums over there, and –" He frowned in concentration, then glanced back at Alison. "String me a bow while I'm gone – as tightly as you can – and find me two or three strong, straight pieces of branch suitable for arrows –" He flashed her a smile. "Sixty seconds, love."

He had gone before she could reply, running down the ramp and over the rock-fall, slipping behind their prison-hut, and round on the blind side of the other building. There was no way in which she could help him now if one of the men decided to come out of the hut. With her heart thumping a drum-beat, she turned to her own delegated task, choosing a whippy, spear-straight length of ash sapling, slightly taller than herself, as the backbone of her longbow. Twine for stringing it was no problem: there were plenty of pieces, in various lengths, lying around on the ground. Notching the wood, so that it would take the cord without slipping, was easy, she did it with the point of a nail; then strung the bow up as tightly as she could. She twanged the tensed cord and it sang sweetly between her fingers. But as a weapon –? She did not know. With shaking hands, she searched the pile of branches for some lengths to use as arrows, tearing off projecting twigs against the grain of the wood ...

And still, that task finished, Stephen had not returned to

her side. Her feverish eyes sought him out. He was in the shade of the Land-Rover, by the wooden bunker at the end of the first hut. Evidently, he had already attended to the vehicle and soaked its interior with fuel, because he now had the lid of the bunker up and was leaning inside, his arms deep in the bowels, his head bent low over some task or other. Alison guessed he was trying to disconnect the pipe-lines of the calor gas cylinders stored there, and she wished he would leave a little more to chance and come back to her before it was too late. But there was no way in which to attract his attention. She wondered if she dare run after him, then dismissed that idea as adding foolishness to foolishness, and concentrated on notching the arrows and wrapping rags torn from Stephen's shirt around the business ends of the shafts. She had reached the stage of dipping these rag-bound heads into the tar in Whoom's tar-drum, carefully avoiding the still unconscious fat man as she unscrewed the cap, when Stephen's shadow fell across her once more.

"All set? Good girl." He twanged the bow string, trying to estimate the pull.

"Is there enough power there to take an arrow across to the truck?" she enquired anxiously.

Stephen nodded. "Normally, yes. I could do it with ease. But I'm not sure how far this tarred rag is going to upset the balance and cause a drag on the arrow. The bolt might fall short."

"And even if it does reach the truck," added Alison, "won't the airstream in flight put out the flame?"

"God knows." Stephen stared at her helplessly. "I hadn't thought of that. Well, that's a chance we'll have to take: I'll make sure the rag is burning as fiercely as possible before I let fly – after all, they won wars with fire-bolts in the old days; burned down cities, stormed stockades –"

"Thank heavens I wasn't around to participate," said Alison with fervour. "And I bet they had a little more going for them than half a shirt and a dab of tar ..."

Stephen leaned over and squeezed her shoulder.

"On your way," he said. "Start crawling as far as the long grass holds out, then wait for the bang –"

"You're enjoying this, aren't you?" she accused, looking at his face. The harsh sunlight showed up the ravages of the past days and, more frighteningly, a kind of glitter in his grey eyes that she didn't like.

"Yes," he breathed. "Oh, yes. And I'd count the world well lost to be able to take a lethal swipe at Ferris –" His glance crossed hers with the flicker of steel, and without another word Alison turned from him and walked to the far edge of the bushes to begin her slow crawl up through the vegetation just above the pathway along the ramp.

It was hard going, worming her way forward, for there were plenty of thistles among the kinder weeds, and segments of broken chalk cut painfully into her knees. The sun streamed down, slashing her head and shoulders with fire. Everywhere, was the drone of insects and the harsher, sawing rasp of grass-hoppers. After a few yards she paused to rest, twisting her head back towards Stephen. He was standing, quite motionless, in the shade of the bushes, the bow held slackly in one hand. Alison crept forward another pace before again halting to remove a thistle from her shin, and, as she did so, a strong arm snaked out from the greenery beside her and, catching her off balance, knocked her forward and down. Quickly, a hand clamped over her mouth, holding her fast, silencing her, and forcing her even lower into the seeding grasses.

Fifteen

"Easy, Miss. Easy," a whisper was saying in her ear. "Everything's fine now."

Alison stopped struggling in sheer surprise. The words had been kind, gentle, reassuring, and spoken by no voice she recognized. She swivelled her head as the hand slipped from her mouth and found herself staring into the face of a young police constable who was lying in the grass beside her. His head was bare, his uniform covered in chalk-dust, and he was looking anxiously at her, his forehead corrugated in a frown.

"Are you all right, Miss?" The voice was a ghost-thread. "I hope I didn't hurt you, but I was afraid you'd call out, or leap up, or something, if I startled you ... Would you follow me?"

Alison did not move. She lay paralysed, staring at him with hypnotized eyes.

The constable dragged at her arm.

"Please, Miss, crawl after me. It's all right. We've nabbed the man on guard at the top. You and Mr Brand were our chief worry – how to get you out of the quarry before the action started. And then I spotted you ... We have the place covered. Can you both follow me?" And for the first time, Alison was aware that Stephen had crept up behind her, and was now resting his chin on her hip. He was eyeing the officer as if expecting him to sprout two horns and a tail.

"It's all right, sir, really it is," repeated their would-be rescuer.

"How did you find out about us and this place?" whispered Stephen.

The young police constable craned down at him.

"Richlyn Taggard. He saw the disposal of Captain Sugden's body and the subsequent search of the Court. The lad had been shooting rabbits in the south wood and was taking a short cut home through the Sugden estate, and stopped to watch some activity with the heavy machinery at the excavations there. Luckily, he kept well out of sight as he'd been doing a little poaching on the side and had a couple of pheasants with him ..." The officer hunched a shoulder. "Anyhow, the boy was sufficiently public-spirited to contact the police – he said the Captain had always been very kind to him – and he told us about the base in the quarry, which was known to everyone around here, of course. But he'd also taken a closer look at that, on the quiet, and already knew it was protected by an armed guard. So we were forewarned. It began to look as if something big might be afoot down here. And once we had grabbed the man at the top of the quarry –"

"Hoat?" put in Alison.

The constable nodded. "After he was taken into custody, he spilled the rest of the story. He told us that you two were below, prisoners, and that at the first sign of trouble you would both be shot. We couldn't doubt that, with stakes as high as they were: at best, you would be held at gunpoint as hostages. We were trying to figure out some way to get you freed before we moved in – and then you did our work for us." He smiled, coaxingly. "So if you will just follow me –" Angling his head, he spoke into his personal radio for a few seconds, ending his message with: "It's all right, I've got them both. They're here with me now ... We're on our way out." After replacing the radio, he said, still smiling: "I'm sure you're bursting with questions, but if you'll just hold them for the moment, I'll fill you in when we reach the top. Now, follow me. You're quite safe. The whole area is covered by our marksmen up there, but we don't wish to start a gun battle, and we would prefer not to alert the men below until we have you safely out of the quarry." He patted Alison's arm. "Don't worry, you're home and dry."

She gave him a wavering smile.

"Ready, Miss?"

"Go ahead," replied Alison, and watched him start off up the slope, sliding forward on his belly, worming his way quickly through the long grasses towards the main track. A smell of crushed chamomile wafted on the air. She made to follow in his wake, then became suddenly aware that Stephen was no longer beside her. Rolling on to one elbow, she looked back along the flattened trail. He was crawling away from her, downhill. Horrified, she stared after him.

For a few seconds she did not understand his motive. Then, quite clearly, as he reached out and once more picked up the longbow, she realized what he meant to do. In an instant, she was after him, no longer caring about thistles and rocks and the pain to her hands and knees. Keeping her head discreetly below the vegetation, and moving as fast as she could, she reached his side and caught at his arm as he struck the first match. It flared and died in his fingers.

"Stephen!"

He turned to her, and never had she seen eyes so cold and implacable.

"Go back, Alison," he said, taking another match from the box.

She watched him fumble with the strike. "No," she whispered. "Oh, no, Stephen. Please. Don't do it. Not now. It's over ... It's all over."

"Not quite." He picked up one of the tarred arrows. "There's still a debt to be repaid."

Alison stared at him. "It doesn't matter. The law will deal with Ferris. Stephen, he doesn't matter."

"He matters to me."

She tugged at his arm. "He didn't really hurt me. Forget it. It's finished. Please. Forget it."

But that he could never do. Ferris had shattered a dream, ruined his world ... Stephen let his thoughts linger on all his lost plans, and on Ardinford – sun-dappled, and drowsy, and infinitely lovely. And, for all time, now, made unendurable to him. No, Stephen could not forget what Ferris had done. Nor did he intend to forgive. Not this, not Dix, not Rosalind – Rosalind, who had never had a damned thing in her whole life ... No, Stephen could not forget that it had been Ferris's orders that had been the cause of the children's deaths, even if indirectly. Nor could he forget the threats and the treatment of Alison. To go through life knowing that, somewhere, Ferris still lived; Ferris, who had taken Alison as a child might take a toy; Ferris, who, if he lived, would still be able to boast, to remember ... No. It was insupportable. Until this moment, Stephen had not realized how fiercely he would resent alien hands on anything of his. He smiled bleakly. In as far as dreams and people and places could be considered his. He set the match to the tarred rag, watched it burst into flame.

"Stephen! No! Please. Forget it. We're all right. We're alive." She stared up at him, seeing herself mirrored in his eyes. A little she guessed what was going through his mind. "Stephen, I'm all right. Michael didn't hurt me. Let him go –" Her voice dropped. "Stephen, please."

He stiffened, and her hand fell from his arm.

"Oh, Michael, is it?" he said in a nasty voice. And she knew then that nothing she did or said would turn him from his purpose. Because how could she explain that she could not have done the things she had and still look on Ferris as a cipher? Equally, now, Ferris was not important, but – she did not want him to die.

Stephen nocked the flaring arrow to his bowstring.

"You'll have to decide on which side of the fence you're going to jump, won't you?" he said cruelly, and with injustice that would later cause him to grow hot with shame. But he bit on wormwood whenever Alison insisted that Ferris had not harmed her, had, indeed, been kind –

and perhaps that was another of the reasons, thought Stephen, why he so desperately wanted vengeance. Illogical, because if Ferris had hurt her -- Either way, it made no difference. His fingers twitched on the bowstring.

For a long moment, Alison stared at him, lips open to plead, the golden light of the day reflected in her eyes, but in the end she said nothing, only turned and began her slow crawl upwards towards the now invisible and patiently waiting policeman.

She glanced back in time to see the fire-arrow fall short and lie smouldering in the chalk-dust. But Stephen stood like an executioner, another missile already nocked in his bow. The flame streamed from the arrow tip, smoking blackly. And then that shot, too, was loosed. It went with a soft hum, like a homing-bee, straight to its target. There was a whoosh and a sheet of fire as the petrol ignited, then a second explosion that cracked her ears; and the whole hut area seemed suddenly to erupt with a roar into a great pyre of poppied flame. The blast echoed round and round the quarry walls, beating up the chalk cliff in fading waves until it died away in the crackle of burning wood. The heat swamped her where she lay.

She closed her eyes against the glare of the inferno, and opened them, minutes later, to flames that were licking steadily lower, only gushing up at erratic intervals as some collapsing chunk of wood toppled and sent up spiralling showers of sparks and red embers which fell like petals over the settling heart of the blaze ...

Even as she blinked, she remembered – and a great many things became plain to her.

The blaze ... Before Alison's eyes there flashed the vivid picture of another fire. November, night, and children dancing round a bonfire on the Green, shrieking, laughing, singing; the smaller fry playing an excited, half-ritual game, outlined starkly by the gouts of gold and orange flame. Overhead, rockets trailing stars.

And November again, but daylight, with Dixon Taggard

performing the same half-ritualistic war-dance around the memorial, waving a clutch of spent firework-sticks, and being abruptly taken to task by Chapworth, the headmaster, for this desecration of the dead.

November still, and the children now standing in silence around the village war memorial, Eric Chapworth, in a flash of patriotism, having decreed that the whole school should assemble to honour the fallen of two world wars. Her own class of six-year-olds there: small frozen faces, small blank eyes, and utter incomprehension. And, later, Dixon Taggard's gravelly voice, unshakably convinced that the numbered slain all lay beneath the granite cross. Alison had tried to explain, had tried to point out the difference between a memorial and a tomb: today, she accepted how little she had succeeded.

Because now, quite clearly, she knew the truth.

Now it was too late, she knew, with certainty, where Ferris's diamonds were; and she knew, with equal certainty, that she would never take them from their resting place among the poppies and the milk-white marguerites.

Down among the dead men. Dead *men*. Dixon had told his sister, so plainly, if only she had understood – if any of them had understood. He had thrown the stones by the war memorial, in the long grass there. On Saturday morning.

And the horse for Rosalind, the cat for Miss Chubb, both with their precious jewelled eyes – the last animals the child had made, both modelled together that Saturday afternoon, before the pageant, in the same place, near the memorial, with the diamonds lying close to his hand ...

Blindly, she turned to Stephen who had come up to her side, moving slowly like a man prematurely old. Was he pleased with what he had accomplished, she wondered? But there was no elation there. He looked merely very tired. Hollow. And suddenly she realized that Stephen, too, was at the end of his tether.

He caught her eyes on him and said harshly: "When this has been sorted out, when we can return to normal, what will you do? Do you wish to stay here, in Ardinford?" He hung on her reply. The magic of the place had for ever gone for him: he would never, now, be able to look at the chuckling river without seeing Rosalind wrapped in her waterweed hair; he would never, now, be able to view the blossoming hedgerows, or the meadows, or the sun on the hills around the village, without the painful memory of these past few days being burnt into everything he saw. Childishly, he wanted to run, wanted to hide, wanted to lose himself in some great amorphous city where nobody knew anybody else, or cared. But, with a sense of fatality, he knew the choice had to be Alison's, she had lost even more than he had, her father and her home at a single stroke, and with a battering of the nerves that would have destroyed a weaker woman.

For a moment, Alison hesitated, knowing it was terribly important that she gave the right answer, that their future happiness rested on her reply. Her own inclination was to stay, to face things out; she was, after all, her father's daughter and had his strength of will and a nature that would fight. But she was also the daughter of Louise, the gentle woman who had captured – and held – Kelvin Hunter's heart and passions even beyond the grave. And she, too, must have been cast in no common mould.

Alison studied Stephen's face. "We'll go," she said, and her eyes held a steady little flame. "As soon as we possibly can, we'll go away from here, if that is all right with you."

His breath went out on a long shuddering sigh.

For some time he had been aware that the air was alive with voices, shouting, car engines, and running feet, and that the skyline was dotted with bustling figures. The outside world was fast moving in to claim them. Stephen glanced back at the fire. Smoke still curled gently from the burnt-out building, but the red heart of it had settled, sifted across with feathers of white ash. It was over.

He relaxed and turned to Alison, but she was not looking at him; her head was down, the bright hair trailing in the grass. And she was crying. Now that it was over, she was crying. At last, now that it was all over, there was time to weep for the dead ...

Wordlessly, Stephen stretched out and took her hand in his.

A FEW CLUES ABOUT MORE GREAT TITLES YOU'LL SOON BE SEEING IN KEYHOLE CRIME

TIME TO MURDER AND CREATE
Lawrence Block

The Spinner had spun his last silver dollar: the Spinner was dead. He was up to his neck in blackmailing and so it was only a matter of time before one of his victims had had enough and killed him.

Assigned to finding the murderer, New York detective Matt Scudder discovered many a strange and cankerous thing about three upright but ambitious citizens who all had guilty secrets to conceal.

DREAM OF FAIR WOMAN
Charlotte Armstrong

A girl falls into a sleep from which she cannot be roused in a Los Angeles boarding house. No one knows who she is until the story hits the newspapers. And then three different people claim she is three different women: heiress, starlet and religious mystic. Intrigued by the mystery, Matt Cuneen follows a tenuous thread of clues back into the girl's past, and uncovers a tale of mistaken identity, unscrupulous greed and ultimately murder.

 Keyhole Crime

DEATH OF A BUSYBODY
Dell Shannon

Lieutenant Mendoza's wife goes to a party to celebrate Sgt. Hackett's new baby and she meets the insufferable Margaret Chadwick — who is found strangled the next day in the Southern Pacific freight yards.

Not a single clue points to the killer when Lieutenant Mendoza is called in to investigate — and he finds himself confronted with one of the most baffling cases of his career.

DEATH AND VARIATIONS
Ivon Baker

Archaeologist David Meynell and his wife are protecting a young American girl from possible danger. They moor their canal boat next to Tongstone Priory and unexpectedly discover the body of former secret service agent Gerald Garland — which triggers a fast-moving sequence of events leading Meynell to investigate the victim's beautiful widow, an ex-mercenary and a railway buff before reality erupts into a classic shoot-out finale.